FOOD CHAIN

FOOD CHAIN

short stories

Janet Kieffer

LOST HORSE PRESS

SANDPOINT · IDAHO

Since this book spans many years, there are many people to thank for help and encouragement in its creation (and some even before its creation). Many thanks go to Bharati Mukherjee and Hilma Wolitzer for joy in the early Iowa days. Thanks also to BBC World Service and Dr. Maurice Lee, and to the Society for the Study of the Short Story. Let me not forget the Bread Loaf Writers' Conference of 1994 (of *New York Times Book Review* fame), and Ron Hansen in particular. Closer to home, many thanks go to Marilyn Krysl, Steve Katz, Scot Douglass for their keen attention to the manuscript, to Alyson Hagy in Wyoming, whose suggestions proved most useful, and to Bob Thompson for his encouragement. Finally, I am deeply grateful to Pamela White Hadas for her suggestions and constant support.

"Sark Lake" *HEAT* (Australia), 2002.
"The Surgeon's Refrigerator" *Grain Magazine* (Canada), Volume 28
        Number 3, Winter 2001. Nominated for Pushcart Prize.
"The Senator's Breakfast" *Mississippi Review Online,* Winter 2000.
"Birds" *Sniper Logic* (University of Colorado), 2000.
"As A Handyman" *Sniper Logic* (University of Colorado), 1999.
"Dust" Joint First Place, BBC World Service Short Story of the Year,
        1997 (broadcast); also published in *Short Story Journal,* 2000.
"Food Chain" *World Wide Writers* (United Kingdom), 1997.
"Wormwood" *The Southern Ocean Review* (New Zealand), July, 1997.
"Dogleg" *Bomb Magazine* (New York), Spring, 1996.
"The Tutor" *The Atlanta Review,* Fall, 1995.
"When Robbie Rockett Died" Roberts Writing Awards winner, *Roberts
        Writing Awards Annual,* 1994. Fiction judge: Gordon Lish.

First Edition

Cover Art *by* Stephen Schultz · Sandpoint · Idaho
Book Design *by* Christine Holbert
Author Photo *by* Don Marchese

LIBRARY OF CONGRESS CATALOGING-IN-PUBLICATION DATA

Kieffer, Janet.
Food chain : short stories / by Janet Kieffer.—1st ed.
   p. cm.
ISBN 0-9717265-5-8 (alk. paper)
1. United States—Social life and customs—Fiction. 2. Overweight persons
Fiction. 3. Food habits—Fiction. I. Title.
PS3611.I444F66 2004
813'.6—dc22   2003028313

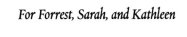

For Forrest, Sarah, and Kathleen

CONTENTS

THE CYCLE

DUST

After Holly saw the hole in her father's throat for the first time, she went down to Shell Beach. She could say "tracheostomy," but she didn't want to, particularly, and so she chose instead to putter and splash in the tidal pools of Indian Point, on the coast of Maine. She squatted above the clear pools and looked at starfish, magnified by the water; she saw the slow-moving green spines of the little sea urchins, and shells shaped like Chinaman's hats with slimy bodies like snails inside. She sat on the sand and popped the air-bumps in the wet seaweed between her thumb and index finger. Her family had come here because her father was sick.

When these discoveries had been made, she seized a dark-gray rock with her fist, and she promptly smashed it against a large, light rock which sat like a statue beside her, and when she did, the small rock crumbled to flakes and powders, sparkling in the hazy sun. She brought what was left of the smaller, darker rock down on the big rock again. It crumbled into flashing splinters and fragments, and some of the dust wandered to her blonde-downy thighs, veiling them in a silver mist.

Her half-brother Jeff said "Ha!" near her ear. He had wandered down from the cottage too, a 15-year-old Downs kid, six years older than Holly, but since he was Downs he was still fun to play with. He wasn't stupid. He had noticed the sparkles. "Fairy dust!" he said.

Holly didn't want Jeff to know yet. Jeff had a way of becoming overly enthusiastic about things, and until she had found out more about the dust she didn't want him around. "Go up and see how Dad's doing," she said.

"It's mica. The shiny stuff in the rocks. Mica."

"Go see what Dad's doing. He can't hardly breathe."

"It's like f-fairy dust."

"Just go, Jeff!"

"OK." He backed up, still looking at the dust. He turned around and climbed the rocks to the cottage lawn.

✦

She followed Jeff at a safe distance, holding a pinch of the dust in her palm. A feral tiger cat ran past and slipped under the cottage, to the dark area under the screened porch. Her mother came out of the screen door to the kitchen in a cotton dress, holding a beer and swaying a little as she walked onto the grass. Holly avoided both of them and used the front door to the cottage and then went into the little kitchen to search its pine cabinets for a jar.

"What are you doing?" Her mother had seen her somehow and was standing right behind her, still holding the beer.

"Do we have a jar?"

"We don't stand on counters," her mother said. Her mother had recently taken to dying her hair a very dark color, but it was now streaked gray at the roots.

Holly found a quart jar with a lid and slid down to her bottom on the counter. Her mother walked toward the screen door and put her hand on her hip. "What are we going to do about all of these cats?" she said. "All of these stray cats! They're likely rabid, some of them!"

While her mother was looking out, Holly took a wooden mallet, the kind used for tenderizing meat, from a drawer. She left the house by the front door and caught a glimpse of Jeff talking to her father, who couldn't talk back, and whose bean-pole shape sat in the small living room, wearing a wrinkled Yankee sort of hat. Jeff made a point, his arms flying in wide arcs around his body, standing in front of a fireplace with no fire.

The mallet didn't work as well as she'd hoped, so she smashed the gray, flaky rock with a harder rock. She selected a big one with a flat upper surface for a work area, and chipped the dark rock into flakes of mica. She ground these to powder with the mallet, and then whisked it into the jar. In the jar it was only gray dust, as it was out in the open when the sun went behind a cloud, but as soon as the sun came out, the powder on the wind or in her hands, it twinkled again. When her mother called her in for dinner, the jar was one-third full.

Her lean father was standing in the middle of some blue-green lobsters that were crawling aimlessly around on the kitchen floor. He made wet coughing sounds like a drain. There was a large pot on the stove, and great clouds of steam rose from it. Jeff was bent over a lobster. He poked at its tail with a finger and its claws flew up into the air. Her father tried to say something to Jeff. His round, gray eyes got big and round, and he made a wheezing noise out of the hole in his throat.

"Don't do that, Jeff," Holly said.

Then her father bent down and snatched a lobster, just in front of its tail, and pitched it into the pot, and Jeff shouted. Her father threw the rest in, one, two, three, and pushed the last one down in with a long-handled spoon, and Jeff began to shake with rage. Her father tried to say something again but only wheezed, and he put his arm around Jeff, but Jeff backed away, shook his head, stomped, and cried "No! No!" Whistling steam noises came from the pot, as if the lobsters were crying.

When the mute man drew the lobsters out, they were a

bright scarlet. He and Holly's mother cracked the lobster shells open with nutcrackers and dipped the meat into cups of butter and lemon. Holly grabbed her jar of dust and followed Jeff out of the house.

It was not yet dark. The sun was low, but still shining, and she took a pinch of the dust from the jar and threw it into the air. When Jeff saw it shine, he smiled again. "Can I do it?" he said. She let him throw it three or four times as they walked around the yard, and she thought maybe he'd forgotten about the lobsters.

But anguish was not far away, for when Jeff threw a pinch of dust onto the bark of a pine tree at the side of the yard, a stray calico cat jumped out from the bushes and clawed his bare legs and tried to bite him. He threw some dust on the cat, shaking it from his leg with some difficulty and said "You son of a bitch!" The calico narrowly escaped his kick and disappeared into the bushes again.

They went down to the beach around sunset. The tide was going out and Holly noticed a big white-clear blob on the beach, shaped like a hamburger. She could almost see colors in it.

"It's a jellyfish," Jeff said.

Holly touched it. Its skin was soft and strong.

They got the bucket from the house, and they filled the bucket with salt water and put the jellyfish in. They also put some rocks and shells and seaweed in the bucket so the jellyfish would feel comfortable. They took the bucket up to the house and left it on the porch. Holly climbed into bed that night when the cats began to howl, looking forward to seeing it in the morning.

Yet when morning came it was time for Holly's father to go to the hospital again for radiation treatments, and her mother started drinking the beers at around 10:00 a.m., and the jellyfish didn't do anything in the bucket anyway.

In the coming days, the children would stick their fingers in the water and feel his slimy body, but even this was a letdown somehow. They went to Shell Beach and collected vacant Chinaman's hats, the ones with holes, to make necklaces, or they stuffed their pockets full of snail shells and walked the edges of the lawn, until Jeff stumbled into the stiff body of the calico cat. The cat was lying on its back, yellow-green eyes open wide, its paws curled in, and its head to one side. Little bugs burrowed among the fur on its milk-colored belly.

Jeff looked at it for a few seconds and breathed hard. He turned to his sister, his face crinkled in happiness. "It was the dust!" he said.

✦

The next morning they woke early and looked again at the dead cat, and then decided to take a walk down the gravel road to Sea Beach, where the surf was louder and the beach sandier. On the way, Holly caught sight of the tail end of a small brown snake eeling through the grass on the roadside. She motioned for Jeff to stay back, and she went to the yellow weeds and bent over the snake. Its head was just slightly off of the ground. It lay still, except for a bright pink tongue that flickered in and out of its mouth, vibrating like a dragonfly wing. She bent over and aimed her fingers just behind its head to pick it up, but it turned and bit her before she could grasp it. She didn't feel the bite, but there were four tiny, red holes on the back of her hand. The snake shot into the woods.

"I have some dust," Jeff said. He felt around in his pocket.

"You took it out of the jar?"

"Good thing I did." He took her hand and sprinkled it over the bloody holes.

"Good thing. He was probably a poisonous snake, but now we have the dust we don't need to worry. As a matter of fact, I know it was a poisonous snake. I could tell by the tongue!"

"Good," Jeff said. He smiled and looked proud for remembering.

When they got back to the cottage, they found the jellyfish littered with black spots, as big and round as quarters. The spots appeared to be both inside and outside his clear, gelatinous body. This seemed like an omen, because the children's mother said their father was getting much worse. Since he couldn't talk, they often forgot he was there. He chose to sit on the plaid sofa in the small living room in front of the fireplace with no fire. At night he listened to the foghorns moaning through the window screens, and there were sometimes tears in his gray eyes that he tried to hide.

"LET THE JELLYFISH GO," the silent father scrawled on a piece of paper with a crayon. He wore the ridiculous Yankee hat. He was almost bald.

They took the jar of dust, and the foghorn blew over and over, aaaa-oooooh-aaaahh!, but there was enough of a moon to show a little twinkling when they threw the dust into the dark air. They dumped some dust on the jellyfish before Jeff threw it and it splashed heavily back into the sea. Then they sat on the barnacled rocks for awhile and listened to the waves and the foghorns before Jeff went back to the cottage. Holly stayed on the dark beach and ground more dust. She could feel the snake bite starting to heal.

✦

When she finally went into the house that night, she found her brother sitting in front of a fire in the fireplace.

Their father was sleeping quietly on the sofa with his mouth open; his chest looked like a deer's when it rose and fell.

Jeff wouldn't take his eyes off of his father. "Give me some dust," he said. She offered it and he cautiously lifted his father's hat and dropped pinch after pinch of it onto his father's sleeping head. It sparkled in the firelight and rolled off of the man's head like sand, into the recesses of the his shirt collar and down inside the shirt, to his shoulders and the back of his neck. His eyes popped open in gray surprise, and he looked at one, and then the other of them before smiling and dozing off again.

✦

Their mother approached them soberly a few days later on their way to Shell Beach, when Holly was showing her hand to Jeff. The gaping holes the snake had made with its wicked and venomous fangs were gone. They climbed down the rocks, and their mother climbed after them.

"He's going back into the hospital to stay," she said, and she said something about how it was serious this time.

"Look," said Jeff. He pointed down the beach, to the sandy part where the waves came in. He began to walk there, and Holly and her mother followed, to where the sea had pushed a jellyfish up onto the sand.

"I know it's hard for you to understand," their mother continued, "and I know you might not want to talk about it, but he might not be coming back. Do you understand what I'm trying to tell you?"

The children looked down at the sand, at a jellyfish clear and healthy, washed up on the beach, a jellyfish with no spots. "I understand," said Jeff. Holly nodded and threw a handful of shiny dust into the air. "He's going to be better," said Jeff.

My mother and father, Amanda and Lou, went in one canoe, my mother trembling like a dragonfly and pointing out rocks in the riffles and chutes between the lakes. Their Grumman was loaded with duffel bags, boxes and tents that were haphazardly shoved under the gunnels. When they got to the big Vs in the water in the faster chutes, Amanda pointed and cried out: "Lou?" and big Lou adjusted his paddle in the stern to avoid a rock suspected below the surface. The water up there got frothy sometimes, and you could never really tell where the rocks were—but the Vs were practical canoeing theory, or at least that's what Corky told me. It was not only that the rocks were there; it was the fact that you didn't know if the canoe would sail right over them or if the rocks would bend the boat like a spoon.

I rode in the other canoe with Corky. I paddled bow, or was supposed to, but most of the time I just rode there, my Keds soaking up an accumulation of cloudy water in the bottom of the boat. The canvas duffels and tents were usually moist due to spray from an errant paddle or a sprinkle of rain, and they smelled like rotten eggs when the sun beat down. A red-bereted guy from Ely (one of the first real hippies I ever saw) had talked us into buying some red tarps, saying that they were good for getting rid of black bears, and that all you had to do when a bear was in camp was to wave a red tarp at it. Corky questioned this, but Lou and Amanda bought the tarps anyway. They said we could throw the tarp over my canvas tent in case

I was stupid enough to touch it from the inside and let the rain come rushing in.

"Paddle, Astra," Corky said sometimes, when the water was static, when we were in the middle of a vast void of water so still that the only ripples were from the startled slap of a beaver's tail. An ear-brushing wind, a hum of insects, some eerie bird song, and the rhythmic plunge-and-drip of paddle into water were the only other sounds. Water spiders skated frantically in the inlets. Corky was somehow related to my mother. He was my uncle, but he was not. He lived in a dilapidated stucco house a few blocks away from ours in St. Louis, was much younger than my mother, and was missing a few front teeth. He smoked a pipe, and sometimes only his two man friends were around, exchanging food stamps and beer. One of them was large and hairy. The other one was small and had the teeth of a beaver. The hairy one tried to finger my underpants one night and I ran away. Amanda didn't allow me to visit Corky's house alone because he was often pickled. "His parents were a little too nice to him," Amanda said, and the way she said "nice" didn't sound nice at all. I once saw Amanda block Corky from passing through our front door one hot St. Louis night, her flowered house dress sticking to her sausage legs, and she said "Damn you, Corky, you are pickled and you are not coming in." And he did not; he vanished beyond the flower clusters on the locust trees and staggered on in the direction of his house, whistling a sophisticated tune. Amanda slammed the door. At random times after that, I noticed brief glimpses of his wild-eyed and grizzled face looking in through the screens of the house. It was said that my grandparents, Amanda's parents, and their parents were farmers in Arkansas who raised cattle and soybeans and fished in the rivers. There was a picture of my grandmother as a little girl sitting in a clear stream just beyond a gravel bar in Arkansas, holding up a crawdad with an expression of wonder and terror. We didn't have many vacations from Corky or from work, but we weren't planting soybeans either.

Corky shook and sweated as he paddled. He had black sandpaper stubble on his face, and he wore a rumpled khaki fishing hat with jeweled and furry flies speared into the brim. Sometimes he pulled out a tin cup and raked it into the lake for a gulp of water or he splashed a web of water across his face. And occasionally, when we went around a bend of a riffle before or after Amanda and Lou, he took out a flask and sampled what was in it.

On one such occasion the riffle turned into a chute, the water started churning, and I began to see Vs all over. I squealed to alert Corky: "We're going to crash! We're going to crash and drown and die!" but when I looked back his paddle wasn't even in the water; his chin had tilted skyward with his flask. The chute was like a roller coaster. The inch or so of water in the bottom of the canoe sloshed back and forth. Monstrous rocks appeared everywhere, like animal heads. I hit one with my paddle to push the bow away from it. When I looked back again in panic, Corky had his paddle in the water. He ruddered us on a zig-zag course through the rest of it. The water finally stilled itself, and he said, "Relax."

At times we floated through shallow waters with swaying green grass, and then just after that we'd find segmented reeds of wild rice that I snapped off and pulled apart to rebuild as necklaces for Amanda, Lou, and Corky. In late afternoons we'd pitch our tents in a mosquito-infested area with a rise of flat land near, or in a cradle of sweet pine needles and deer droppings with a breeze, water rushing over large rocks nearby. Twilight was the time for fishing, and I had my cast reel with a worm I'd pierced in bloody spurts on the hook, or some white pieces of pork rind, but Amanda, Lou, and Corky had fly rods. Corky fished with grace, his line like a melody or a poem, his fly barely touching the water. The shrieking loons began to sing.

Amanda pan-fried bass, northern, and walleye in the iron skillet in the evenings. I watched Corky clean the fish precisely, with the long blade of his hunting knife, after some steadying swigs from his flask. He first cut the spine of the wiggling fish, right behind its head, and he cut the head off. I was free to use the walleye heads as puppets, and I did, because the eyes on the walleyes could see in all directions. They talked to each other from my hands.

◆

One day there were no riffles or chutes between lakes. We had some kind of destination the whole time, and I didn't know what that destination was, but we were headed there. We spent a lot of time hauling the gear. We came to a swamp. Corky and Lou had to consult maps to figure out where to go. Amanda looked at it, but they waved her away.

"Goes north," Lou said.

"A portage through a swamp?"

"It goes north, and here we are, and we have to go through it. That's what the map says."

"Fuck," Corky said. He sighed and hoisted the canoe over his shoulders. A loud, complicated bird song echoed all around us. Amanda said it was a hermit thrush.

Amanda lurched behind Lou through the swamp. I followed her in my cutoffs, the water up to my knees, and Corky followed me with the other canoe, looking like a surreal and stretched out snail. We had to haul boats, shelter, stinking fishing gear, and Bisquick. The trees in the swamp were skinny and deciduous, without the striped bark of the birch. No watercress existed in the swamp, and I was not allowed to drink any water there. It was a nasty and mysterious place, and I half expected to see white-dead, bloated bodies surface or the Creature come. Amanda's calves sluiced against thick water, water full of life in its green and moldy parts. Minnows pelted my ankles. Amanda looked back beyond me with the dark rolling eyes of a horse.

To get through a swamp, you have to pick your legs up very deliberately. I hauled my legs up out of the muck on the bottom, but it only revealed little dark worms that had attached themselves to me in the water. I couldn't brush them off. Corky set his canoe in the swamp water and put his canvas pack into it. The water had only reached my knees, but his cold hands inched up to my thighs and squeezed them. "Get away from me, Corky!" I said, and I fell back into the rancid water.

"Whaddya mean?" he said. He looked hurt and helped me up. He took out his flask and poured some whisky or whatever alcohol on the place where each leech had attached itself to me, and they were easy to pull off this way, though they stretched like rubber sometimes before they relented. He smiled his missing-tooth smile at me, and I thanked him. Ahead of us, Amanda and Lou had stopped to deal with the leeches, and the four of us continued on among the skeletal trees of this murky womb.

We escaped this place and were supposed to portage around a beaver dam, but we were so tired that we got out of the canoes and hauled them over it, my feet cracking the scrawnier sticks of the dam and my legs sinking into it.

✦

It was almost dark when we reached our next dot on the portage map. We couldn't see much, but this was supposed to be Sark Lake. We didn't build a fire and we didn't eat. Corky, Lou, and Amanda pitched heavy tents and unrolled the sleeping bags. Lou raised our enormous food duffel, with its can of beans, oil, iron skillet, and Bisquick, up to a high branch of a tree. I had my own pup tent, and Corky helped me pound in the stakes and tighten the lines, his lips sucked in where his front teeth were missing. "This should make a fine little place for a girl like you," he said.

Sometime during the night there came a crunching of rock and needle outside my brown tent. In half sleep I could have sworn that someone actually parted the flaps and looked in, but I couldn't be sure. I remember sitting up, listening without being entirely awake, and lying down again. I can't remember if I was fully asleep or not before I knew it was Corky, but I sat up again and saw the shadow of him peering in at me through the parted flaps. The shadow disappeared. After that I couldn't sleep, even though there were no more footsteps outside.

Pretty soon I had to pee and I crawled out of my tent with the flashlight. I relieved myself behind a little pine tree near the water, and something splashed in the water of the lake, beyond the water fall; that is, you could hear it over the waterfall, and I wandered, following the gold illumination of the flashlight. A sound like Corky's whistling came from the other side of the lake, but I was tired and I couldn't be sure if that's what it was. In spite of this, I found myself exploring, and when the path of the flashlight hit a series of stones going up a mossy bank, up I went. It was a ladder of rocks. You had to use hands and feet to climb it. When I got near the top, I tossed the flashlight upward, and the wide beam of light landed on a moose skull somebody had wired to a tree. I crawled up to a plateau on my knees and stared at it. Getting a grip on the flashlight revealed other wonders. Crude rock pews sat before a stone altar, the dark eye sockets of the moose skull overlooking everything. A loon wailed from a distant part of Sark Lake. Then there was a noise like the slight bending of a wicker basket, the snapping of soft pine needles, and Corky emerged from behind the altar. He sat on one of the pews. "Interesting place!" he said. He was pickled. "Come on over here, Astra, and sit with me."

I had no intention of sitting there with him. I pointed my flashlight at the moose skull one more time to look at it before climbing back down the rocks.

✦

The morning brought a great fracas to our Sark Lake camp. Amanda banged a pot and the iron skillet with a spoon in front of a black bear who hung its head like a shamed dog. Somehow the bear had gotten to the duffel bag in the tree, and some remaining Bisquick lay scattered on the ground. Flakes and dust of Bisquick clung to the bear's paws and mug. Amanda was too close to the bear, I thought, but like those animal enthusiasts who join animal rescue shelters and really don't know what they're doing, she decided she should approach the bear with a banging of pans and shame the animal as you would shame a dog. "Get out of here!" she shouted, and she whopped the spoon against the pan. At times I wanted to rescue Amanda the way she would not rescue me.

When I first saw Corky that morning, in the middle of all of this, Corky hung his head in the same way the bear did. I looked back at Amanda, who was still shaming the bear, and at my father, who joined her by shouting at it. It was an amazing creature, and it reacted to my mother, but not very quickly. It languidly pawed the air. I remembered the red tarp, found it in the packings of my parents, and shook it wildly at the animal, who pretended to meander before high tailing it through the woods, into the water, and toward the protection of a distant shore. We watched its head bob as it swam away, the remnants of Bisquick on its body no doubt dispersing to feed the tiny, special organisms in the virgin waters of the Quetico.

This was a dramatic beginning to any day. We didn't have much in the way of Bisquick left, with which Amanda had hoped to fry up some sugar doughnuts in hot oil over the fire, but we still had bacon from the cooler, and we had our fishing rods.

We caught a lot of fish that day. I don't even know why Amanda, Lou, or Corky bothered with fly fishing; anything you threw into the chute between Sark Lake and whatever lay beyond would yield some fish—I could cast with my live bait and fish would bite at every fifth cast or so. I tried to cast into the quiet and hidden places; this is what Lou had taught me in Missouri and it worked in Canada also. As the treacherous rocks lay in hidden places when we traveled the waters, our food lay there too; but our food moved around as the rocks did not.

The fishing was so good, in fact, that we decided to stay for another day. I was secretly enamored with this idea since I wanted to climb the steps to the sanctuary again sometime when Corky was busy doing other things, or at least when he wasn't pickled.

✦

It wasn't long before I thought I could control the weather. The Quetico was like no place I'd ever been before, and I had some kind of special bond with it and all of its creatures and plants, even the frightening ones. Proof of this lay in the fact that my breasts had started to puff out a little—only on the ends, and I knew damn well that the Quetico had something to do with it. I could bid the skies to offer rain or snow, and after lunch I jumped from rock to rock on Sark Lake, begging the skies to be kind, remembering the immortality of the Moose near the altar. I yearned to explore a small, misty island that graced the middle of it. I was an idealist, albeit a dirty one, and Amanda interrupted my dances and told me to take a bath. She gave me some Ivory soap and a towel. I asked her if I could have an empty canoe to practice with (as long as I was down there in the water), and Lou brought me a canoe and a paddle, shaking his head. He walked back up the trail to our camp. I stripped, my young girl belly sticking out, and I hesitated. The water was cold. I waded into it, naked, climbed into the canoe in the shallows, and paddled stern like an expert, I thought, heading for the middle of the lake. I dared myself to paddle to the fairy island and back again, and naked at that. The Ivory soap dirtied itself in the bilge on the bottom of the canoe. When I was halfway to the island, I heard the thin and paltry voices of Amanda and Lou. When I looked back, I saw their bodies, stick men on the shore, and I also saw Corky gawking at me over an expanse of weeds or brush, away from my parents, like an evil character from a picture book. I kept paddling, imagining myself a sort of female Viking with a horned hat, my blonde hair flying in the breeze. My arm muscles and back felt good. Plop, stroke, feather (drip); plop, stroke, feather. I was doing pretty well. I was going in a straight line toward the island. When I got close, a baby bird caught my attention. It was yellow and fluffy, but spotted; the closer I came to it with the canoe, the harder it cranked its webbed feet to get away. You could tell it had webbed feet by its speed in the water. A gull circled my canoe from above, pelting me with dung. The fuzzy bird disappeared into an inlet or crack in the island, and I was left to find something else to do. So I threw my paddle on the shore and rocked the canoe until it tipped over, and then I swam under it and went inside. Water light lines reflected on the inside of the canoe, and any noise I made resulted in a metallic, echoing, chamber sound. After awhile the canoe wanted to tip itself back upright, or so it seemed to me, but this was fine since the air was getting thin. I got the uprighted canoe into the shallows of the far side of the island and found Corky there, soaking wet, holding my paddle, staring at me. I went back into the water until it was up to my neck, and his eyes trailed my body. His mouth was open.

"Give me my paddle, Corky," I demanded.

He looked as if this wasn't the reaction he expected. He said, measuredly, "A little girl should not paddle so far away like that. It ain't right. Anything could've happened to you."

"Give me the damn paddle!" I liked saying damn paddle at that moment.

He didn't say anything for a second. Then he said, "Only if you paddle back right now."

"Did you swim out here?" I asked.

"I can swim back."

"No, Corky," I said. "You can paddle the canoe. I'm the one who's going to swim back."

He took off his sopping shirt and tossed it into the water. When I put it on, the hem of it hit the bottoms of my knees. "Paddle back," he said. "I'll swim."

✦

Somebody had been using my casting rod. When I got back, after I'd gotten chewed out by Amanda and Lou, I thought I'd toss a few lines into the chutes and try to catch a big northern. If they wouldn't let me paddle where I wanted to, at least they ought to let me fish. I also considered using my wiles at controlling the weather to get even with all of them, but that wouldn't have helped. A raging thunderstorm wouldn't benefit anyone, least of all me if I happened to touch the inside of the tent, inadvertently, in my sleep or something.

The reason I knew someone had used my rod was because there was a lure on the end of the line. As I said, I didn't use lures; I used worms or pork rind. The lure was a treble hook, but that's not what I found alarming: the terror came when I found that the red and white, flashing spoon lure actually had a drawing of the Devil on it. It was a classic Devil rendition, with pointy horns and a goatee, stamped on the red and white side of the lure. I snapped the line with my teeth and took the lure up to the Moose Skull Church for further examination. It wasn't until I'd climbed the rock ladder and sat on a cushion of pine needles behind the altar that I wondered if there was any connection between the Devil lure and the Moose Skull Church itself. Maybe the very place in which I sat had some cultish and Devil aspect. It was right around this time that I heard Cory and Amanda and Lou, below, involved in some kind of argument.

It turned out that Amanda had found Corky's flask, or found Corky drinking from it, or some such thing. I spied on them from my elevated position, but I could only see Lou through the pine trees. His fat arms flailed wildly in the air. Voices echoed around rocks and trees, and you could only make out certain words, but booze was one of them, and Astra another. This outburst had stilled even the birds; it had stilled me, until I saw Corky move into view, heading toward my father with the long hunting knife he used for cleaning fish. Then they shuffled behind some trees again, and I could hear them scuffle, shout, and swear, and Amanda swore too.

"Corky!" I shouted. "Corky, come on up here!" The noise below stopped. I saw Lou come into view in the gap in the trees, stand with his hands on his hips, and look in my direction without knowing where I was. And soon the hard sound of boot on rock came, and Corky's head, with the jeweled flies of the crown-like fishing hat, rose over the bank where the stone ladder was. A red creek of blood ran on his face. I'd planned to run when he approached, but he wouldn't look at me, and for some reason I stood, riveted, staring at the sparkling flies on his hat. Then I stepped toward him and gave him my bandanna.

We'd only planned on a few more days of this Canada business, and I wanted to keep going, but I had my doubts as to whether Amanda, Lou, and Corky would feel the same way. They couldn't smell the pines the way I could smell them, and they couldn't control the weather.

I went to the top of a bluff overlooking the lake. The sun was starting to go down. Near the shore, two bears nuzzled each other, and one bear jumped and pumped on the other bear; the bear who got jumped on seemed oblivious. It was motionless and looked drugged. The bears stayed entangled for some minutes, and then they parted and went their separate ways into the trees. A moose visited the shoreline like a shadow puppet. It sniffed and pawed at the water.

A thick beaver dam held the body of lake water back, and a round beaver house hulked on the opposite shore. If you squinted in the needled sunset, you could see beaver heads gliding through the stillness of the water— but just as soon as you spotted them, they quietly disappeared, leaving their ripples. The water was a long way down from where I was standing, maybe fifty or sixty feet. I kicked off my Keds, took a breath, and dived.

ECLIPSE

Consciousness isn't like a light switch that goes on or off.
It's more like a dimmer on a light.
—*Nathan Cope*, American Anthropologist (1986)

Wade is dead, but Willa forgets. She forgets her dog's name, or that she has a dog; it is a Sheltie that barks at what used to be Wade's feathered hat. The dog thinks the hat is a chicken, or maybe a pheasant. At the gathering after her husband's funeral, in her house, the dog barks at the hat rack. She claps her hands and laughs with delight, and says, "Where did that cute little dog come from and what is he barking at?" It's the night of a lunar eclipse.

✦

Willa sleeps through earthquakes with epicenters close to home. Her round blue eyes flutter in rapid eye movement under wrinkled lids as she dreams about laughing with Wade and kissing him, while the ground that supports her bed jolts, ripples, shudders, rearranging her long white hair. Even after she picks up splinters of glass from framed photos which have fallen off walls or jars of applesauce, shattered and spewed on the pantry floor, and sometimes as she is doing these things, she forgets about the earthquakes, even though she may remember for a fraction of a moment when she sees an avalanche of mud in the neighbor's swimming pool, as she has seen on and off for forty years. She remembers periodically that something is "soft," as she puts it, pointing to her head.

"Where is Wade?" she says, and then remembers that he's dead. Her blue eyes overflow with tears, and she claps a hand over her mouth. "I'm so sorry!" she says, as if she has offended someone. And she becomes distracted by the dimensions of the world around her, and forgets again.

◆

Mimi is from Palo Alto. She is bejeweled and drunk at the dinner table. "I don't want low income housing in my neighborhood," she says. "We worked hard to get where we are. It's not fair." An olive drops from her mouth onto her plate.

Her tiny husband is embarrassed and leaves the room.

"For awhile we thought we'd have to live here in the valley," she says, tracing a wide arc in the air with her arm and nearly slapping the face of Wade's elderly lawyer, who is sitting next to her.

The old man nods, pretending that Mimi did not almost hit him in the face. He eats paté with a spoon, and shakes his head in disgust and says, "Poor bastard wants his ashes flown to St. Louis. It says so in his will." Silvery paintbrush tufts of hair bloom from his ears.

Willa is in the hall next to her bedroom. She squints at old photos on the wall and becomes agitated, as if remembering something. She looks at her veiny hands and frowns, and then enters the bedroom to rifle through boxes and drawers. The dog follows her in, then comes back out again, his toenails clicking on the tiles in the hall.

Willa's forty-year-old nephew, Alex, is standing in the driveway with a friend, smoking a joint, holding a box a little larger than a ream of paper under his arm. "I thought we'd spread him under the olive tree," he says, his voice croaking through withheld pot smoke. He gestures toward the backyard. "We planted that tree together when I was ten."

"So he was cremated?" asks the young male friend.

Alex exhales finally—a whispery ahhhh!—and holds up the box. "Yeah. He's right here. So we're going to spread him under the tree, because he always liked that particular tree. I just decided to do it."

The tree has symmetrical, full branches that weep toward the ground, and it looks especially picturesque to the dope smokers in the dim light that comes from the house.

The moon is almost gone from view but will reappear, brighter.

Taking the joint with an exaggerated couple of nods, the younger man widens his eyes at the box as he inhales. "Cool," he says.

"Calcium," says Alex. He goes to the lanai to set the ashes on a table there.

Someone starts to play a Grieg concerto on the piano. The dog barks at the hat rack.

"Have you ever tried to maintain a swimming pool?" Mimi is growing louder and has attracted a wide audience, some of whom are seated at the table and others who have drifted in from other rooms.

An eight-year-old boy named Stephen shakes his freckled, shaggy head. No, he seems to say. Willa has given him her fox stole and he is examining it, especially the head and whiskers. He can't wait to show it to the dog.

Mimi brushes crumbs from the linen tablecloth. "Well it's hell, and I mean hell, and that means you have to pay somebody to do it, and half the time they don't do it right, screwing up chemicals and leaving dead frogs in the water—"

"Mimi." Willa has approached the back of her chair and is tapping her shoulder with a fist. "Mimi!"

Mimi tries to wave her away, coming once again dangerously close to the lawyer's face, but her hand stops in mid-air close to his cheek. She sways in her chair for a moment, staring at the table.

Willa looks at the back of Mimi's coiffed head with wide blue eyes. "She stole my jewelry! You always wanted my ring, and now you have it! You just took it!"

The crowd looks elsewhere in embarrassment at the outburst and the piano goes mute.

"Poor bastard," says the lawyer.

But Mimi is still staring at the table and she starts to cry. Large tears roll over the translucent, wrinkly skin on her cheeks and drop to her hugely bosomed, flowery blouse. "What do you say," she says, "to a woman who cannot remember how to sign her name on a check?" She looks at the lawyer, and then at Stephen. "A woman who puts laundry detergent in the dishwasher and foams up the kitchen?" Her tears turn angry and her bloodshot, green eyes flash, going from face to face. "Who can't remember that her husband is dead!"

Willa leans over, bumping Mimi and spilling her bourbon, and picks up Mimi's Gucci bag from the floor by her chair. She opens it and digs around inside, making purse-searching noises of keys and pens and make-up cases. She pulls forth a twinkle of a diamond ring and holds it high for all to see.

"Well thank you," says Willa, righteously. She gives Mimi back her Gucci bag. She puts the ring on and stares at her hands.

Mimi's tiny husband ushers her, with some difficulty, from the room and leaves the house from the back via the lanai. Stephen follows them, stroking the beady-eyed fox stole, and pauses where the outside door of the lanai meets the driveway. In the backyard, under a brilliant three-quarter moon that nobody notices, two men are on their hands and knees under the olive tree, brushing mulch back from its trunk.

Willa joins him there. "Why is Mimi leaving the party?" she asks. "And where is Wade?" She wanders over to a glass-covered table where she finds a box about the size of a ream of paper. Smiling, she picks it up and shakes it. "It's heavy!" she says. "Like it's full of rocks and sand!" She peels back a corner of the brown wrapping paper.

Alex, having finished his mulch clearing, brushes off the legs of his pants. He and his friend share a little pipeful of pot, and he is ready to retrieve Wade's ashes from the lanai and spread them under the tree. Should there be some kind of significant ceremony? Should he light the tiki torches and call the guests? He decides against this, and heads toward the lanai to retrieve the ashes.

As he is doing so the concerto starts again, from the beginning; the Sheltie barks at the hat rack, and Willa abandons the box to run back into the house. "Say," she says, beaming at the dog. "Whose cute little dog is that, and why is it making such a racket?"

BIRDS

L ike an old animal now, I want to be by myself—
like a lioness scraping back snow with splintered
claws to find dry straw-grass, chewing cautiously.
I sniff around. The one exception to this is my granddaughter, Lizzie.

Gwyn finally came to see me. She brought her Lizzie,
and they entered the kitchen where I'd let the tomato
soup to burn on the gas stove. Somehow I forgot about
it. I had taken my wool dress and socks and underwear
off and was out in a modest snow, feeding the birds. As
God says of the sparrows, "Truly, I say to you, not one of
you is arrayed such as one of these." This is true. And He
didn't even mention the cardinals. I must have looked
like a skeleton draped with a rubbery cloth of skin, my
old breasts barely hanging on by tendrils of tissue paper.
I dumped the Folgers's can of sunflower seeds into the
bird feeder and dropped a handful. They peppered the
blinding snow. My daughter was bewildered and disgusted
with me, but my granddaughter was delighted. When
Gwyn lectured me about the charred soup and about my
nakedness, Lizzie went outside, took off her clothes, and
imprinted a snow angel of five-year-old proportions right
into the back yard. Her green eyes are wise beyond their
years. I have such love for Lizzie.

✦

Just after Axel died, fishing in the trout stream close to
the house, some generation Xers, dressed in nylon, found

him face down in a shallow part of the stream. His face had made a sculpted imprint in the amber-white gravel. He wore his fishing vest and clutched an orange red fly very close to his heart. Axel was not my first husband, but he was my only husband. His mother had lived in a small sterile house, a spooky house, and Axel was scary, in a way. You never knew what he would do when the lights went out, but he was my friend, and feeding the Midwestern birds was one joy we had together. After his body was gone I never forgot that.

I know what I did after Axel died. People think I don't remember because I was in such distress, but I remember some of it. I challenged them with the double-man saw, and I wept as I hurled the scythe at them, at Chip Landcroft's bicep, at Madie Andersen's head. Madie was wearing a stupid derby hat. I remember how the pig-faced Kathy Velmont took me to see hairy old Dr. Histerling, and Dr. Histerling looked and felt my body up and down on the sterile table and announced that I was feeling anguish and stress. The truth of the matter was that I was experiencing grief, and not only grief, but a desire to be numbed for the rest of my life. I got so drunk I didn't know what time it was when I woke up, so drunk that I didn't wash my underpants or brush my teeth, and so drunk that I needed more water than I could swallow. The house became distorted. I had kept clean linens and curtains before Axel died; I had kept the counter wiped, and I'd snipped roses the size of grapefruits with my pruners to put into vases now and then. But after he died, I found myself surrounded by the dry flurry of dead flower petals and pollen, the stick of butter or jam on the kitchen counter, and the dead animal smell of regular bad laundry that cowered in the corners of the house.

So I painted waterfowl in the kitchen. I painted mallards and their various environments—watercress, pond, and cattail with attendant red-winged blackbirds against a backdrop of cream yellow. It was impressive. I noticed, sometime after I was finished, that the ducks had a gleaming, elfin aspect to their eyes, and that they seemed to be watching me. That could have been my imagination.

After that I cleaned up the house. I am still forgetful. Things have changed, but I am not a disorderly drunk. What I do I do with a loose kind of purpose, but a growing one. What is there left for me now? There is Gwyn, or so I thought just before Axel's funeral, when I was still out of it, when I wore my Ray Ban sunglasses, black crepe dress, and old lady shoes. Gwyn had to dress me, and during the dressing I noticed the uncanny change in my daughter, an eerie metamorphosis that was almost as bad as Axel's death.

Her very pregnant body lumbered, like a cow, up to my upstairs bedroom in the farmhouse. I saw her coming. I had had too much to drink and was lying on the unmade bed, searching for smells of Axel. She put black panty hose around my bony ankles and I protested, grabbing at the bumps on the chenille bedspread with my fingernails.

"You're not an animal," she said. "Get dressed and have some coffee." She literally scowled. I hadn't seen anything resembling that expression on her face since she was two.

"I wonder," I said, "which one of us is the animal, and which one of us is susceptible to change, and which remains the same?" With which Gwyn found an old shoe of Axel's and tossed it from the inside to the outside of my bedroom window, shattering glass like ice.

I didn't make it in to the memorial service. I can't remember exactly what happened, but I do know that Gwyn left me in the car outside the church. She tilted her long nose up into the air and disappeared into the narthex with her policeman husband, Leo. She clutched his arm ceremoniously and was gone from me then. She was with Leo and the growing fetus in her body.

A crow cawed from the steeple of the stone church. It wasn't too long after that that I felt a little better.

✦

A few days after Lizzie was born, Leo brought her to see me. "What the hell did you do to this kitchen?" big Leo asked, turning around and around, clutching the little fruit-like baby so hard I thought that she would burst.

"I decorated it," I said. "May I see the baby?"

"Oh. Yeah. Sure." Leo held her out to me like an offering, still gazing at the kitchen walls, doors, and ceiling. "Gwyn's not feeling too good. I figured you'd want to see Lizzie."

"Is Gwyn all right?"

"Yeah. She's okay, basically. But she's tired and a little weird. She doesn't like me too much now. She's not sick or nothing."

I took the baby from him. She was wrapped in a quilted baby bag, with a shoestring tie around her face, and she struggled inside it. Her eyes rotated wide like planets in their sockets, and she looked at me. She pummeled the bag, just as strong as you can imagine.

"Does Gwyn like her?" I asked.

Leo quit looking at my duck paintings. He put his hands on his broad cop hips and stared at me. "Of course she likes her. She loves her. That's her baby. Lizzie's her baby!"

The baby made smacking sounds with her lips. "I know, Leo, but you said she was a little weird."

"Well that's only temporary. She just had a baby, for god sakes."

"You want a beer?"

"No. And neither should you." He looked at the kitchen décor again, but I could tell he was only pretending.

"I don't want one. I'd like some tea though. Could you make me a cup? That way Lizzie and I can get acquainted." I didn't wait for an answer. I took Lizzie to the old sofa Axel and I had bought thirty years before, and we sat down and talked. We talked about taxes and what various birds liked to eat, based on where they lived, how they flew, and the designs of their beaks for cracking nuts or chewing fruits. Chicka-dee-dee-dee!

Leo emerged from the kitchen with a can of Bud for himself and a cup of tea for me.

"I still can't believe you did that weird thing in the kitchen," he said.

"Does it scare you?" I asked. I untied the shoestrings of the bag and freed Lizzie's head. She smelled milky and clean, and she had tufted, bright orange hair. "Look at this darling's hair!" I said. "Leo! Look at this!"

"Why should the weird thing in the kitchen scare me?" he said. "Should it scare me?"

"Leo, look at this child's hair! She's an angel!"

Leo said, "You're not listening to me. You're not listening on purpose."

I had to put effort into remembering the history of the conversation. Then I said, "The ducks in the kitchen?"

He swigged his can of Bud. "Yeah. That's what I was talking about."

"Oh, I did that recently. It was therapeutic. But look at this baby, Leo!" I moved my ancient hand close to her gold-orange hair. Static electricity made it barb out like a dandelion.

◆

The disrobing, the taking off of my clothes is not a rebellious act. When Gwyn reprimands me for doing this, it's her rebellion again, I think, or her reaction to a situation she herself has essentially created, going with Leo, abandoning me, as some grown children feel they must do to survive.

But Lizzie is mine, and I hope that until she's ten or so we can sneak around outside in the crisp periphery of the farm under a tent of stars, pretending that the one-armed man I hired to feed the horses is still alive and that we must avoid him, pretending trout still live in the stream and Axel is still after them with his rainbow flies, and pretending that we, ourselves, are capable of flight.

TUMBLEWEED

It had once been a farm, with a few horses, cattle, pigs, and crops that struggled in dry and blowing dirt. And her father had been a farmer who fashioned crude irrigation pipes in wheat and soy fields, and who plowed with a tractor flaking rust. His wife tried to endear herself to him by making him dependent, and to an extent that worked; as a girl, Diane heard the creaking bed but in the light of day her father was only polite, and that was when he was sober.

✦

The farm hung vacant in the ragged dusk of Indian summer afternoon. She scaled the stairs to the front porch. Her father wobbled naked in front of a dirty window, an unhappy clown in a dark comedy. She knocked on the frame of the screened door and called to him.

The timbre of her father's screech of reply echoed through the house and out the screen.

Everywhere she looked was gray and white and tan. The haze of the sky matched the color on the house where the paint had peeled away. Tan weeds struggled up between the separated boards of the porch. "It's me," she said. "Food shopping today."

"Leave me alone!"

"It's me."

He had put on a pair of stained boxer shorts. "What are you doing out there on the porch?" he said.

She took a dusty chair and began to scrawl out the usual grocery list on a piece of paper bag. Her father liked things embraced in cans. He liked canned stew, baked beans, canned peaches and pears, Campbell's soup. He rarely ate much of it; he rarely ate at all—when he did it was out of a can with a bent spoon. It was the vodka he relished, and now he quivered like an oak leaf with the wanting of it, and his red-rimmed eyes jerked aloft, as if expecting a flock of birds or a shooting star.

"If I get you soup, it'll be vegetable soup," Diane said.

The old man's eyes traced something along the width of the ceiling before he looked back at her and said "Hmmm?" He focused on her for a minute. "What happened to you?"

She didn't want to explain again because she knew he'd forget. She was just beginning to show and her body was bloated, the pressure of fat and liquids against drum-taut skin.

"What happened to you?" he repeated. "Looks like somebody rammed an air hose up your ass!" She cried a little and a tear and some watery snot dripped onto the piece of paper bag with a soft tapping noise. She crumpled it into a ball in one fist and rose from the chair. "I'll get the usual," she said. She let the torn screen door slap shut and an animal scurried around under the porch, digging and scratching. When she was back on the dirt and weeds and almost to the truck the old man shouted, "Bastards ain't always boys!" and she left him to his hallucinations, his shapes in the mist.

✦

When she came back he was rioting through the tall weeds in back, by the persimmon trees. His arms circled down and out and up until he embraced the bleak sky, swearing words she could not understand with the melodic voice of a preacher or a politician. She left the food and the vodka on the chipped Formica table in the kitchen and tiptoed down the warped cellar stairs.

A bad rendition of her mother stared out from the corner, a portrait; the artist had not captured anything about her mother except for the expression in her eyes, which was outwardly a deer-in-headlights expression, but which simmered with a desperate manipulation. Her mother had always starved herself before Diane was fifteen, but at around that time her mother grew and grew, rounder and rounder and fatter and more grotesque in her obesity, as if the years of starvation for the sake of popular flowerdom had finally accumulated to the point where her mother tried to make up for lost time with boxes of doughnuts and platters of meat-laden spaghetti. But this portrait was painted when her mother was still painfully thin, when the sorrow and manipulation were the most noticeable, when her mother had been hungry and angry and had masked it with something which was supposed to pass for sadness or martyrdom. The artist had painted black hair, the color her mother had dyed it after it started sprouting gray at the roots. She was a vessel of secrets. Low autumn light slanted through a flat cellar window and illuminated the portrait with a gold tone, and the character that passed for her mother gazed at Diane, hollow-cheeked, an angel of questionable sacrifice.

Ironically, the brown-eyed woman's death had been a secret from the rest of the world—supposedly sudden, at home, in bed, with almost no clue or cause. But she had gotten into Valium, and when that wasn't enough, had eaten enough animal tranquilizer to drop an Angus bull (which by this time she almost resembled). Diane's father had insisted on constructing a rude wood box for her coffin, made by his own hands. With a couple of coats of fragrant varnish and some twinkling brass hinges, he insisted this was at least as good as the wood boxes at the undertaker's, drunkenly declaring the business of death a conspiracy, and the little town actually let this slide. At this time Diane noted that her parents had left each other in their staying together, and that it didn't matter which went first. Nothing really mattered.

✦

Berta was one of those people for whom Diane held a horrid fascination, who had flunked in grade school, and who towered in near-adulthood over the rest of the class. Her house was down the street from the school, a large two-floor box of screenless windows, splintered wood, and progeny, with skeletons of vehicles and appliances in the yard. Berta was slow. She had a rusty voice, and when she spoke it cracked. She was a big girl and had been pregnant by the time she reached the tenth grade. She tapped Diane on the shoulder when both were in line for prenatal vitamins at the clinic, and she looked exactly the same as she had five years before, except that her face had deep pock marks where pimples had been, in skin like oatmeal. In her still-cracking voice, she asked about Diane's baby, and each sentence ended with an upturn.

"I'm just beginning to show," Diane answered. "You can't even really tell."

One crack, "Hnngh!" signaled a giggle from Berta, who patted a stomach that looked only fat, and she said "This is my third baby. I hope it's a girl." She nodded up and down before and after she said anything—this too had not changed. "Who's the father?" she said.

"Clyde Hennessey," Diane said. "I don't know if you know him."

Berta nodded up and down, strings of oily brown hair

dancing on her shoulder, and said "Yeah!" She picked
something from her scalp and flicked it to the floor.
"Hnngh! They say we're supposed to stand in this line
and get our pills. I want to go home."

"Do you still live over by the school? Or did you
move?"

"Yeah! Hnngh!"

Berta got her vitamins first and clodded out of the clinic
ahead of Diane. Diane saw her begin to walk in the direction of home and saw her stop to pick a giant sunflower.
Berta tugged and tugged on the thick, hairy stem until it
popped and she stepped back. She pressed the dry-yellow
bloom against her cheek; teardrop seeds fell to her feet,
and she continued down the road against fields of wheat
and corn.

✦

Diane passed the paved road turn-off to the college on
her drive back to the trailer and remembered when she'd
taken courses there, before she'd moved in with Clyde.
She'd taken introduction to botany, among other things,
and she could not now look at a navy or garbanzo bean
without thinking of a cotyledon and how the sprout grew
from the middle of the two halves of a soggy seed. Her
quest for higher education ended when she met Clyde, as
if his company dictated that she was on the Wrong Road
in her life, and being with the round and carefree Clyde
was where she belonged. She was still content, but passing the paved road made an empty place in her stomach,
and she felt suddenly sleepy, as if she wanted to retreat.

She was surprised to see Clyde lounging on the couch
when she went inside. He watched a daytime talk show,
and the trailer reeked of dope and dirty socks. She
mentioned her surprise.

"No work today," was all he said, and he gazed at the

television with raw, glassy eyes. He picked up a pack of Marlboros, lit one, and hacked the smoke out.

Sparks of anger exploded inside her but she said, "You can only do what you can do. Still, we got to save for this baby."

"Babies don't cost much. You're going to the clinic," said Clyde. Somebody from the trailer park was picking off prairie dogs with a .22 in the field next to the park, and it caught his attention. He looked outside.

"They cost more than I used to make at the drug store," she said.

Did you pick up the food stamps?"

"No. I was with the old man today, getting his food with his money."

"Did you get us anything? With his money?"

"No, he doesn't have enough."

"The hell he don't. He's rich. He's just fucking tight, that's all."

She didn't say anything to that, but she remembered Berta. She said, "Clyde, me and you are going to have to talk about something."

"What?"

Someone on the talk show got irate and cried, and Diane went to the TV and turned it off. "I said I didn't want to get married, but I decided now I do."

For a minute, Clyde was still as a mouse. Then he waddled over to the little refrigerator and opened a can of beer. His back was to her. "We never said we'd get into that," he said.

"I know we didn't," Diane said. She sat on the couch and began to cry.

He turned around and said, "Now don't start that. Don't start making me feel like an asshole, because I'll leave."

But she knew he would not, and she knew they'd get married, and she knew these things although she'd never say them aloud. She only sort of knew them, on the inside.

✦

So Diane cleaned up her father's house, and she found him something to wear, and she found a thin Baptist minister who was willing to marry them in the church, and they made ready for a little reception in the back yard of the farm after Clyde had mowed down all the weeds. Diane flew into action with the telephone book and a pen. Her father had said he would pay, so she ordered flowers, a wedding dress with pearl beads and lace, fold-out tables and a tent for the yard, and a pig they could roast on a spit if Clyde would do the honors of arranging it. She invited couples, only couples, from the drug store from where she used to work and from Clyde's assortment of construction buddies and drinking acquaintances. And the old man sat and watched most of this from an upholstered wing chair, which was losing stuffing from its arms and wings, drinking vodka-on-ice from a jelly jar.

When Clyde went in to join him she stood in the yard with her hands on her hips, trying to picture where the table should go and where Clyde would put the spit for the pig, picturing a dream-like flurry of couples, some of whom already had children and would bring her baby gifts like rockers and swings and disposable diapers. Her thoughts were leaning toward cozy nights in the trailer with Clyde when she caught a glimpse of Berta through the trees. Berta was lumbering down the road in front of the house, her shoulders hunched over, looking at her feet. As if on a dare she cranked her head to the right a notch and peered through dirty hair at Diane and at the yard. Diane pretended that she had not seen, but eye contact was all Berta needed. She came stomping up to the house.

"You and Clyde moving in here? To your dad's house?" she said.

"Hi Berta. No. We're just planning our wedding reception. We're just getting the yard ready."

"Hnngh! Hnngh-hnngh-hnngh!"

"What's so funny?"

"He wounnent do that for me." The big woman's expression changed. Her eyes darkened and contracted, her cheeks puffed out, and she looked like a bulldog. She put her head down again and walked to the road. A big tumbleweed, of amaranth, bumped up against Berta's ankle and stuck to her leg. She shook it off and it was airborne for a moment before hitting the ground again, to tumble off into the corn stubble of a neighboring field. Diane looked up at the house. Through a window, she saw the gray back of her father's head and saw Clyde looking out. Then his face disappeared.

✦

The couples wheeled down the dusty road in Chevy and Ford trucks, on Harleys, a few of the women in tight jeans and high heels that Diane admired in her pregnancy. Clyde was stoned for the wedding and reception, but Diane didn't mind so much. None of the twenty guests seemed to notice; they helped themselves to the keg of Coors and the pot luck side dishes of baked macaroni, cucumber salad, and the roast pig from the spit. Clyde enjoyed these foods. Diane's friend Lucy switched up in her tight jeans and punched the dirt-grass with red high heels, and she presented him with a three-tiered wedding cake with a figurine bride and groom on top. Clyde looked overjoyed. Someone had hauled the old man's favorite upholstered wing chair onto the grass; he slept with this head against the left wing and his upper lip twitched from the escaping stuffing there.

Diane looked over to the table where some presents were stacked. Some were wrapped in newspaper, others in formal wedding paper, and some were decorated with duck-head safety pins. This was when she saw Berta. Berta picked up an especially frilly present, shook it, and sniffed it. She wore a T-shirt that stretched tight across her breasts and her belly and which bore an arrow pointing down and the word BABY. She drank from one of the plastic keg cups, licked the foam from her lips, and shouted "You dinnent think I'd come, did you?"

Somebody turned down the tape player, and the only sound was a baby's whimper and a country mother cooing to quiet it. Diane scanned the crowd for Clyde and saw him frozen in a stoned horror, a piece of wedding cake half in his mouth, black crumbs of chocolate on his round chin.

"Well I got his baby too!" Berta said. "Look here, says baby! And I don't get no presents! And I don't get no party! What do I get? Hnngh! All I get's a bastard!"

The old man woke up. He rocked himself laboriously out of his chair and stood on the grass, swaying. "Bastard?" he said.

"That's all I get!" said Berta. All of the couples were watching her now. The men looked relaxed and entertained. The women cast weary glances at each other.

The old man pointed to Diane. "Well she's a bastard. Or she was a bastard. You don't see me complaining, do you?" He fell back into his chair and settled.

Diane's blood raged. Clyde was fat and useless, and she wanted to strangle him. She went into the house and down the stairs to the cellar, where the other women could not direct their pitying stares. But she could not escape the eyes of her mother, and she again looked at the masked face, this time wondering about the root of the anger there. The portrait bathed in the early light—pathetic, helpless, secretive, strong.

Clyde's boots thumped down the stairs, and she turned to him. He still chewed a piece of wedding cake. She blinked hard at him and said: "I know that Berta person is lying, Clyde. It's all just so hard to take on my wedding day. Just so hard to take." Clyde narrowed his red eyes at her.

Diane felt the baby kick and roll inside of her when she and Clyde walked upstairs to rejoin the party. Berta was gone. She walked up a small hill, which gave her a view of big sky and surrounding farms, and still there was so sign of Berta. She looked down at the yard and saw her father, a dead-yellow man in his chair.

Days later, when her baby at last tore her and thrust its egg-shaped head into the world, Diane had the uncanny image of her home in her mind. Dark storm clouds covered distant mountains, and the wind kicked up a tumbleweed of amaranth. It rolled endlessly on past the field of grass or of crop, or the barren field, past the gnarled claw-shape of lone western tree; it bounced and spun and tumbled on forever through the gold-barren landscape of the Plains.

FOOD CHAIN

I never believed in any of that evolutionary crap.
Or how we are connected with the animals.
—*Bob Hopkins,* salesman

There's something about waking up and not knowing where you are for a minute. The stale air conditioner smell and the hard bed alert you to the fact that you're in a hotel, but you don't know where.

If it's light enough you can see where you've thrown your shit on the floor, your briefcase might be on a table, and still there's that institutional hotel air conditioner smell. You might remember where you are by the clothes you threw on the back of a chair, or by a phone book on the shelf of the bedside table with the lamp. Then you know: "I'm in Topeka!" or "I'm in Little Rock!" or "I'm in Juarez!" But you really don't know for sure until you've taken a shower and shaved and put on a clean pair of underwear, and you think about the day before on the plane or making the presentation, or having a dinner with a pretty thing somewhere that you'll put on your expense account. It's all business. Wherever you are it's exciting, doing business, and that's what you call it, and it's even exciting to realize that you don't know where you are, there in the dim morning on the hard bed.

You get to pad down colorful carpets to the elevator and go out for bacon and coffee and eggs, reeking of aftershave and wearing a Rolex.

When you're eating your bacon you don't think of the pig. You just eat it.

You get to wear suits with pants pressed by an automatic pants presser right in your room. If your suit isn't clean, well fuck, call somebody on the phone! They'll take it and clean it and bring it back to you, no problem.

That's the way it was at first, when I was selling most things.

The food business was different.

✦

Harv Espy was digging into a mountain of dead pigs with a fork lift. There was a heat wave in the Midwest that summer and thousands of pigs had died. Lots were dead on the trucks when Espy got them. He'd throw the forklift into reverse with a shovelful of deadweight pigs and the wheels would spin on the dry dirt, and then he'd jerk forward to some big crates in the back of the place. He dumped them in there, where they were hidden. Their short legs looked like matchsticks when they fell.

"Rendering plant'll come and get them," Espy said, when he got down from the forklift. He wiped his head with a bandanna.

He looked rough. "We don't kill pigs here," he said, deadpan. "We kill sows and boars." He said everything like that. He was the guy I was trying to sell my prods to, and he was a true stoic. Espy wore sunglasses that wrapped around his head, and a plaid shirt and baggy work pants, and underneath I bet he was all ribs and elbows. The bald part of his thin head was shining in the sun, all sweaty, and what he had of hair was cut real short.

An old farmhouse with peeling paint occupied part of

the premises. I noticed it when I was talking to Espy. A woman's head appeared for a second in a window with a torn screen. It was a wide, plain face.

"How much money today Harv?" the woman shouted. She was disturbed. "Pigs eat better'n we do!"

Then it disappeared.

He didn't say anything back to the woman but he looked at his shoes with crossed eyes. "No pigs," he said again, monotone. "It's like I tell the animal rights people. It's all in the food chain. You got producers, you got consumers." He lit a filterless smoke. "We all gotta feed somebody."

He thought nothing of it too, because he ordered pork sausage when I took him out to breakfast at a truck stop. "Patties," he said to the fat waitress. "No links," he said. Then he ordered an Old Style to go with it. He still had his sunglasses on.

I ordered some eggs and some crispy bacon. "Business is like that," I said to him. "Like a food chain. Especially when you're in the food business."

✦

Espy sat at his desk in a little office that looked like a house trailer. There were flies all over the place and periodically he'd try to snatch one out of the air. But that only works when it's cold. And it was so hot that his little window air conditioner wasn't doing anything. "So why should I buy from you," he said. It wasn't even a question, because there was no uplift on the end of it. It just stopped. "I got another company'll sell prods to me for less." He tried again to snatch a fly. He had his chin resting in his hand and the hand was yellow, like jaundice.

I considered open and closed probes, the Ben Franklin close, and the quality spiel, but I didn't think any of those would bring Espy out of his shell, so I opted for the win/win approach.

I cleared my throat. "So Harv, if we came close to matching their price, and you knew our prods would last longer and work better, you'd recognize that as a win, wouldn't you?" I said. I was playing it by the book.

He sighed. "I really don't know what the hell you're talking about," he said.

"What I mean is, you'd be a winner in that situation, don't you agree?"

He leaned back in his chair and it creaked. "What would I win?"

"Well shit, Harv," I said to him. "You'd win extra savings, buckolas, denaro, for your company. You'd save a lot. And that would make you a winner, wouldn't it?"

"I don't know if I'd go that far," he said.

"Sure it would! Hell yes! You'd be a winner, and I'd be a winner, and that's what we call a win/win business transaction, or relationship. I can tell you're a shrewd businessman and that you'd recognize a win/win when you saw one. Wouldn't you?"

Espy started wheezing and hacking and spat into the trash can. He waved a fly from his face. Then he got up from his chair and waved to me. "Come here," he said.

"Where?"

"The kill floor," he said, like he was disgusted with me.

✦

We were at the chutes when the trucks pulled up, and I told some jokes I'd heard about fat women on account of the waitress at the truck stop. I guess I was nervous because I'd never seen a kill floor. Never seen one since, either.

Espy didn't laugh. He waved at the trucks. "There's a lot

of money in there, if they're alive," he said.

The backs of the trucks opened up and hundreds of mottled gray pigs came barreling down the ramps, trying to escape the heat in there. They were happy to be out, and wild eyed, and they were big fuckers! Eight hundred to a thousand pounds, some of them, all hooves clattering down the ramps.

They ran right into the chutes.

✦

The chutes are wide at first. Then they get narrower. That's when the pigs slow down in a kind of bottleneck, and that's where the prods come in. There were a couple of guys on either side of the chutes and all they needed to do was get one of the prods close to a pig. The electricity arcs bright blue, right to the pigskin, and you can hear it, zzzzttt! You don't even have to touch the pig with the prod. Sparks fly right out. Thousands of volts, a lot to us, but these were big fuckers.

That's what they told me at work before I went to these pork people to try and sell the prods. To try and do a little business.

Big pigs have big lungs. And they yell big as a man, and shit bigger, when they get hit with the arcing spark. Jesus, Mary, and Joseph, you would not believe the screaming. "Weeeeahhh!" and louder than somebody my size, and then another "Weeeoohh!" and pretty soon four or five were doing it at the same time on account of the prods. And the electrocuted ones kicked their back legs into the air and then tried to climb over the ones in front of them, where the chute narrows, but the ones in the very front were taking their time, although there were guys with prods up there, too. It was a queue of pigs. They eventually made it in to be shot and killed, but there were pigs jumping all over each other in pig hysteria, hoofed and twisty-tailed, trying to get away from the shocks.

And then one popped up right in front of me. He threw his front legs over the bars of the chute, with his front hooves dangling over on my side, and his snouty head with the pig eyelashes. You could tell he'd been shocked because he had shit himself. He was in a frenzy, struggling and wiggling as hard as he could to try to get over the bars, his back feet whipping up off the ground. Then he stopped trying. He realized he couldn't make it over. The chute rails were the barriers. He knew.

I looked up to where Espy had gone to kill the pigs, way at the front of the line. He saw me looking at the pig. His eyes had that same crossed expression they'd had after his wife yelled at him. Then he disappeared again in the midst of the whole operation, in front of some pigs and guys.

The pig shook his head and his ears flopped. He looked at me.

✦

They say pigs are smarter than dogs and I'm here to tell you it's true. That pig knew he was going to die. He'd gotten 10,000 volts in the ass at half an amp, and his comrades were being prodded and stuffed into narrower chutes and then shot with the stun gun before having their throats slit. They were wallowing in their own turd to their own deaths, and this pig, staring at me, he knew it too. The other pigs were still screaming.

His eyes were pleading with me to get him the hell out of there. He knew that if I didn't help him, he wasn't going to make it out. He didn't know what ham was, or links compared to patties, but he knew he was going to die.

He was near the end of the whole rush, and a lot of the other pigs ran past him.

Espy was way ahead where they shoot and kill the pigs, his wife on his back and dollar signs in his eyes.

The guys with the prods were ahead too, with the other pigs, and hadn't noticed my pig yet. They would notice him soon.

There was no way to pick the fucker up, or hoist him over the bars of the chute, so I jumped in there with him and his sewage, in my shiny shoes.

My Rolex fell off somewhere in a pile of pig crap, I don't know, but I ran back up the chute towards the trucks. Guys were shouting and swearing behind me but I kept going. The gate was leaning against one of the ramps and I threw myself against it so hard I almost snapped a hinge. That the pig was running after me was a given, I knew how smart he was. Besides, you could hear his galloping hooves.

I held the gate open for him and he streaked through in a gray blur. He got side tracked in a little corral to the right of the trucks for a few minutes. He ran around and around in circles, with fire in his eyes, hell-bent and determined.

Espy came out, walking jerky like a string puppet. He was spattered with blood. He didn't have his sunglasses on and he had dark, cavernous eyes. "What the hell'd you do that for," he said. Even though he was pissed, his voice sounded the same.

My pig charged through a gap in the corral gate. He tore out to the other side of the road and into a gold hay field and zig-zagged around bales, little rectangles, still running.

One of the prod guys was standing next to me and I didn't even know it. He had long hair and was wearing Espy's sunglasses. "Wow," he said. "I never knew they could run like that."

We watched the pig disappear into the trees just beyond

the hay field, a little speck vanishing into a thick, green forest.

♦

You never know what the future will hold.

One Tuesday morning a woman called me on my office phone. "Bob Hopkins," I said.

"Is this Bob Hopkins?" she said.

"That's my name!" I said, and I smiled, because if you make yourself smile when you're on the phone with somebody, you always do a lot better. You never know when it's going to be a fucking customer or something and you want to be prepared.

"This is Marlene Espy." Her voice was real low and slow. "I need to talk to you about my husband."

I had to rack my brain to figure out who her husband was, but the last name made my stomach feel bad, and I finally figured it out. "How is Harv?" I said. I have a good memory. It had been months since I let out that pig.

You could hear her start to cry. "He's missing, Mr. Hopkins. The last I saw him was two days ago, headed out the door with the Remington 12-gauge, said he was going to find the pig you let out, because he could use the money, sell it for chops and ham."

"Hell Marlene, that was months ago. How the hell'd he think he was going to find it?"

For a minute she didn't say anything. "I don't think that's what he was truly going to do," she said. "You know, Mr. Hopkins, ever since that day you came here and let the pig out, Harv has been distracted."

Personally, I thought Espy was distracted all the time, but I didn't allow as how to her.

She started again. "He said you set it free, and he started going on these jags of weeping and crying and such," she said. "And he started talking to the pigs."

In business, you never see failure as failure. Because that's not what it is. Failure is what you think it is, but it's really a chance to develop your sense of humor, or find a learning experience, or to practice your techniques and perfect your performance. It's the game you play to win.

So that's why I went to Espy's place again, even though he had chased me off months before because I let out that pig. One thing you have to do to be a highly effective person is to do things you don't really want to do. I was playing the game to win, so I went to see Marlene.

Besides, I hadn't earned my commissions. Guys were always trying to get me out to the kill floor, and I wouldn't go. I figured with Espy gone, Marlene might give me a sale. And after her phone call, a visit was the least I could do. The food business was different than business I had done before.

I pulled up the dirt drive in my Caddy. There were three black and white police cars outside the place, roughly at the entrance to the chutes, and some cops standing around, and also some cops walking around in a cornfield next to the one where the pig had run off to.

A sheriff approached my Caddy when I got out. He was your generic sheriff, chewing gum. "You looking for Espy?" he said.

"Just dropped by," I said. I didn't want to tell him I'd talked to Marlene, and I hoped to hell she hadn't talked to him about me. I looked around. Some guys from the kill floor were oozing out from there and joining the cops in the corn rows to wander. "I stop from time to time to do business."

He snapped his gum and looked toward the field. "You won't do any business today. Espy's missing for over a couple of days now."

A wide woman with mouse brown hair stood next to the sheriff's car. Her face was blotchy and swollen like she'd been crying. Marlene.

"What?" I said. But I didn't fake the concern altogether. The Espy account was my last chance at a commission or else I would be tossed on my ass out of the food business. "Where'd he go?"

The sheriff stretched. He looked tired. "Last time anybody saw him was when he took off across that field looking for a pig that escaped a couple of months back. His wife said he went on a rampage and started walking in that direction with a twelve-gauge under his arm." He looked at Marlene and then said out the side of his mouth to me, "I think they're having some money troubles. Maybe he just booked, you know?"

"You never know," I said. There were now all kinds of people crashing around in the field. The sky was already a clear, dark blue, the cornfield was yellow, and the people looked like insects penetrating it. The police didn't want them there and tried to wave them away but it didn't do any good.

Marlene set out to join them, moving slowly, because she was so large and sad. She had an ugly yarn shawl wrapped around her shoulders. It was the color of her hair and it looked like she had made it herself. Her dress was like a bag, and it was brown too.

The sheriff watched her. "She doesn't know what she's doing," he said.

✦

She was a faceless, brown hulk transversing the corn. She looked like she was swimming when she made her way through the stalks, looking down. She bumbled over to the far side of the field. Some other people had started trickling back but the cops were still there. They weren't looking for anything anymore and were standing around with their arms crossed, talking the way cops do. After they had talked for awhile, one of them went to get her. I suppose he had decided they wouldn't find anything.

When he got about halfway across the field she started jumping up in the air waving her arms. She was making a sorrowful noise. It was low and deep and loud and we all started running to her. I ran behind the sheriff across the road and down the corn rows. It seemed like forever before we got to her, and I was out of breath.

She stood there with her face buried in that ugly shawl with Espy's body at her feet. I saw the pigs, and I bet it was the same son of a bitch I let out, him—or her I guess, and a family. There was one big one and a few smaller ones. Some of the pigs had little tusks. They all backed up and blinked at us. They had been eating Espy.

Marlene rushed at them, making the same low sorrowful noises she had before, first at one, then at another, and they pounced in reverse like on springs. She chased the big one into the trees. Bare branches snatched at her yarn shawl.

Espy's head was blown apart in back. The barrel of the Remington stuck out from underneath him. You couldn't even recognize him except for his clothes and his crooked elbows. Smaller animals, little ones from the ground, the trees, and the corn, they had been eating him too.

CONSUMPTION

THE PRESIDENT'S GIRLFRIEND

When I hit forty, they didn't want me in the sales job anymore. I could have sued them for age discrimination but when I talked to Mason, my lawyer, he said that it would be hard to prove. He said that they hired women all the time for sales and it had something to do with sexual wiles, and while I denied to Mason that I had ever propositioned anybody to make a sale, I knew what he meant. One of my personal improvement books is written by a champion woman of the economic and illustrious 1980s. She says that it's OK to flash a little leg to make a sale, but you don't want to sleep with anybody.

All I did was smile a lot and take people out to dinner with my American Express, and explain what we had to offer. I didn't dress like a tramp but I tried to look sexy and business like at the same time. That's part of being a woman and has nothing to do with trying to sleep with somebody. The eighties was a boom time and a real time for women because they made those soft suits with the short skirts, and those suits meant business. But like I said, when I hit forty they said they were downsizing but they weren't. After they got rid of me they hired a thiry-year-old. Her body wasn't the same as mine. My body had changed; it had grown sagged and distorted like a lump of warm cheese, and it was a lot bigger than it had ever been before.

I polished my interviewing skills and I went on interviews for sales jobs. I did everything you're supposed to do: I smiled all the time, I looked enthusiastic, I sat forward in my chair, and most importantly I didn't let the interviewers take control of the conversation. This is especially important for positions in sales and marketing, and it's one of the personal 7-step goals as outlined by Steven R. Covey. I believe in him the way a recovering alcoholic believes in AA. Steven R. Covey: *First Things First*. I got his books and his tapes. Thanks in part to Steven R. Covey, I had been making seventy grand a year. But then the bottom dropped out. The interviewers said my closing skills were weak. They said my specific sales experience did not match what they were looking for. What they really meant was I was too old because I was forty. That is what they meant. I tried to use visualization techniques to picture myself back in a size ten dress, but that doesn't work too good if you are forty and used to taking people out to dinner all the time. Picture yourself sitting by a linen tablecloth with real silver. Picture yourself with sparkling jewelry that is also fashionable, and imagine yourself as a role model you'd find in a women's magazine as a business character you'd die to emulate, and that's what I was. I'd fall asleep dreaming about the deals I might make and resulting life changes I might enact: a large house with huge closets full of shoes, a bidet, a swimming pool, and hired help all the way from grass mower to kitchen mopper. I even imagined their faces: the grass mower's face was a nineteen-year-old, north European male with sparkly eyes, while the kitchen mopper was a short female Asian averting her gaze.

I used to go to the gym and keep my body toned, because it was part of my career, but when I neared forty I got both busy and tired. I just didn't give a shit anymore. I know the women's magazines tell it like it is, especially the career articles about how to keep in shape and how to talk to your boss, but I just didn't care. No one would hire me because I was forty.

So I went to an agency. The woman at the agency, Jill, was twenty-eight years old and she herself was in sales, in a way, because in addition to placing people, she had to sell people to companies. She sent me out on a few sales job interviews and I got kind of excited talking with her. We discussed the *One Minute Manager* and *Teaching the Elephant to Dance*, and *What They Teach You at Harvard Business School*, and those sales and marketing gurus, Steven R. Covey and Tom Peters. She had more tapes than I did and we agreed to trade. Jill even had video tapes. And she told me that if you listen to Mozart it improves your mind and you can make more money. I went and bought some Mozart.

But it didn't work. Mozart took me to some strange places, it is true, but I didn't get any smarter. The next thing I knew, Jill was saying she didn't have any sales jobs. She asked me if I would like a temp job as a receptionist to help pay the bills. She didn't have anything else, and I wasn't getting any sales job interviews, so I took it. It would only be for awhile, and I could still go on sales job interviews.

The first time I sat down in the receptionist chair and put the headphones on I thought I was going to cry. Being a receptionist is a very demeaning job. People yell at you on the phone, and they yell at you when you transfer calls, and they want to you go shopping and wash the dishes. I had been making seventy grand (or would have, on my commission schedule), but I was suddenly relegated to a peon role. At first it made me sick to think I was a receptionist. I didn't even want to go to my high school reunion. People always ask what you do. So I didn't go to the reunion. I had to take the messages and write them down on the WHILE YOU WERE OUT pink pads. I, who was used to having those messages taken for me.

"I'm not really a receptionist," I'd tell people, salespeople, who were waiting to give presentations to the executive VPs. "I'm just doing this until I can find a satisfactory position again in sales—one that is a good relationship and complies with my lifetime goals." A couple of the women didn't believe me, I could tell. They were very well dressed and had expensive briefcases and shoes, and they were in their thirties. I was tempted to tell them what was going to happen to them, that the same thing that had happened to me would happen to them, but I didn't. They smelled like Sunflowers perfume and wore the same kinds of sexy suits I used to wear before I had to buy big baggy ones.

I'd been a receptionist about two months when I first saw the president. I didn't know he was the president. He came up and stuck his fist into the candy jar on my desk. One of my responsibilities as the receptionist was to fill the candy jar. He liked caramels, and so I got lots of those, and pretty soon I had created a little stash of them in my bottom desk drawer, in case everyone else had eaten the ones in the jar. He looked just like all of the other guys—conservative suit and tie, shiny shoes, that sort of thing. He even smelled like the other guys. Until I was a receptionist, I never noticed how much alike the guys in the workplace seem. When I was in sales they all seemed different, but when I was thrown into the role of receptionist, they all looked alike.

He had a head of thick white hair and I remember thinking it looked funny because his face looked so young, and he had these black-rimmed glasses that made him look like something out of the sixties or early seventies. He kept pushing his glasses up on his nose even when they weren't slipping off, so the effect was like a guy just hitting himself in the face all the time. It was really funny. I thought maybe he was in sales. It was surprising I noticed him at all, considering how alike the guys looked.

I remember how the realization hit that I was attracted to him, seriously attracted. In the first place, it was difficult to talk when he was around. I kept losing concentration, like there was a big fog in my head that kept pushing me to the floor. And I had a tremendous urge to look at his face from about three inches away. But I couldn't do that. That would be ridiculous. I found myself squirming in my receptionist chair. This wasn't a conscious action on my part. I'd catch myself doing it, cough, and then grab a pen or a pencil. I'd pretend to write something down on a pad of paper, and I wouldn't look at him then. That could only make an embarrassing situation worse.

◆

The president had his own direct line, and his own private secretary, and the secretary had real red hair and was about twenty-five, while here I was, with my hair dyed henna and I was forty. This comparison sticks out in my mind. It says something about how women see other women when there's a man involved, and it was after I learned he was the president.

Once I answered the phone while he was standing next to my desk. He had just come in and was shaking out his Eddie Bauer umbrella, and a phone call came in for the president, and he saw me there wearing the headphones, and I miserably said, "Mr. Schnorberger is the president, and you'll have to call his direct line." He heard me say this and he held a finger up, signaling me to hold the line. He took his rubbers off and took the phone receiver and said "This is Chuck Schnorberger." I just about died. Here I had thought he was in sales.

But he was smiling at me during that entire phone conversation and he must have seen the surprise on my face. I pretended to be involved with some mail, and he ran his fingers through his moussed hair. I almost fell out of my chair. I could tell he liked me then. I could tell he had noticed me.

✦

Jill reminded me that when you are looking for a job, you are really selling yourself. Sometimes people buy things just because they like the salesperson. But it's especially true in any kind of career search or job change. So I didn't see maintaining the president's attention as anything more than a good career move, on one level. I didn't see it as setting out to deliberately make a sale by sleeping with him, as the woman in the personal improvement book had said, but rather, I saw it as a sort of sampling of the product. The product, in this case, was me. Repeated sales calls serve to reinforce a product in the potential customer's mind, and so wandering upstairs in the vicinity of the president's office didn't seem like nefarious behavior to me. It seemed natural since I'd been in sales.

This was hard to do, of course, because I was expected to answer the phone. I enlisted the human resources director and had her answer the phone while I went to the bathroom and then went up to where the president was. This worked out nicely because I could put on makeup or brush my hair in the bathroom right before I went in the vicinity of the president. The human resources director was a mousy character and I had no problem with her as competition, but the president's personal secretary was another matter altogether. I couldn't figure out how much the president liked or noticed her. She was about thirty years younger than he was, and she had freckles and one of those tall, athletic bodies. She read romances at her desk when he wasn't looking. I didn't really know what type of guy he was or whether he would go for that sort of thing or not. There were moments when I felt terrible for my impressions of her. These moments passed, and everything was on the surface once again.

It was not clear whether or not the president had a wife. He didn't act like he had a wife, but from my career in sales, I know that means nothing. Often guys that don't have wives act like they do have them, even, and I think this type of guy is the shy type. Some guys are hard to categorize. Later I learned that he did have a wife, but he didn't live with her. They were separated. But it didn't matter much.

There I was in the demeaning job, and there was the lonely president, and our paths just happened to coincide. Like a character in a romance novel or a women's magazine, when I saw him notice me, I was determined that he should not be lonely anymore.

Once when I was outside of his office, talking to his secretary about the weather, I thought I saw him wink at me. He was on the phone, as usual, but he was looking at me and I'm pretty sure he winked. The next day when he passed my desk I was sorting the mail and he asked me out to lunch.

"What is your background?" asked the president, when we had sat down to our Mexican food. He was having a margarita, but I chose not to drink. If you are a receptionist and you drink at lunchtime, you practically fall asleep when you go back to your desk for the afternoon, because the job is so boring.

"I have a background in sales," I said. "That's what I usually do. I am actually not really a receptionist." I purposely did not order a taco because they are messy.

"No, I mean where did you grow up? Where have you lived?"

"I have lived in various places because of my sales career,"

I said. "Sales often involves transfers. My husband—well, now ex-husband—could never really handle it, how we moved from place to place and how I didn't mind because I loved just being in sales."

The president cleared the salt from the rim of his glass so he wouldn't get a mouthful of it when he drank. "So you're not married?" the president said.

"No," I said. "It gets in the way of my career."

"Where have you lived?" The president was all eyes. He wouldn't take his eyes off of me.

"Oh, Florida, Jersey, Boston, other places," I said.

"When you were in Florida, did you go swimming? On the beach? In a bikini? You like the how the water feels?"

"Yes, but not often, because I was so busy with my work. I was a great closer in Florida. In that particular job, I was selling juicers to grocery stores. And you can imagine the market in Florida."

"Were you married when you were in Florida?" the president said.

"Technically, yes," I said. "But I had separated from my husband—well, now, ex-husband. He just could not handle how into my job I actually was. I sold so many juicers down there, it would have made your head spin. I was a dynamo when I lived in Florida."

The president's eyes got even wider. "I'll bet you were!" he said. "Are you sure you wouldn't like a margarita?"

"Oh, no thank-you," I said. "Of course, I was a dynamo when I lived in Boston too. In that particular job, I sold shrimp de-veiners and other things that have to do with the seafood industry. You would not believe the amount of business I racked up at the Boston Seafood Show. In that show, I wore a sort of costume to attract customers."

The president's face brightened. "What kind of costume?"

"Well, you can imagine," I said. "There aren't many

women at the Boston Seafood Show."

"Describe your costume. What did it look like?"

"It was sparkly, mainly. But I racked up hundreds of thousands of dollars worth of business at that show."

I suddenly remembered that the president had virtual control of the conversation. I had been answering questions. So I took a new tack. "What kinds of trade shows do you participate in?" I asked.

The president bit into a taco and lettuce and beef and sour cream splotted onto his tie and shirt. He shook out the napkin that had been in his lap and wiped it off.

"Oh, several," he said. "You can come on into my office and I'll show you some pictures. We had an award-winning display last year for two of them. But our display might be even better if you agreed to wear your costume."

"Let me tell you a little something about marketing," I said. "You have to know your audience. You have to know your market, and what appeals to them. And so the costume I wore at the Boston Seafood Show might not work well at these specific trade shows you are talking about."

"But we won't know until I see it, will we?"

It was pretty clear then that the president would do just about anything to see that costume, or see me in the costume. It was obvious he was a very lonely man.

✦

I got a paneled office with mahogany furniture and a real credenza, and a Pentium, and the title of Acquisitions Director. The president felt that if I had been such a whiz at sales, I might be that much wiser as a supervisor of buyers. He was right. I could tell when we were getting hosed, and I was good at my job, and I didn't have to be there all the time, as long as I stayed with the president a few nights a week. But people knew, and people talk, and they started calling me the president's girlfriend. I never quite got used to that. It reminded me of what the woman had said in the personal improvement book about women in sales, and I was frightened when I realized that I couldn't even remember her name.

One night when I stayed with the president in his luxury condo, he wanted me to perform oral sex on him. For some reason that night, I just could not get into it. I didn't really love the president, but I liked him a lot, yet I had never had this specific problem before. Men had gone down on me in cars, in kitchens, and on dinner tables next to roast beef sprigged with parsley. But I just didn't want to get near him at all, let alone that near. It had never bothered me before, and when I saw the president hang his white-haired head in disappointment, I started to cry. But this I hid from the president. He pulled himself together and put his glasses on and hit himself in the face several times, and then he went into the living room to sleep on the sofa.

I didn't see him again until the next day at work. He must have sneaked into the bedroom to get his clothes without waking me, because I slept until nine and didn't get into my office until about ten. I sat at my desk and looked at some buyers' reports, but I didn't really see them. I was waiting for the president. I did not want to see him, but I knew he would appear.

✦

At a little before noon he wrapped his neck around the corner of my office door and just stood there looking at me for a minute. He didn't say anything. He looked at me the way he had the day we went to the Mexican restaurant. And then the head disappeared and he was gone. I wondered if I should go to his luxury condo that night, and I didn't go. I went home to my apartment and ate a box of Kellogg's granola and went to bed. I was exhausted and scared, like a bird who has crashed into a window. Are women supposed to be scared when things like that happen?

The next day he came to my office early and he didn't say anything again. He was wearing a Christmas tie and it wasn't Christmas. He came over and started to massage my shoulders, and I couldn't stand it. He was like a foreign animal and I couldn't stand even to be near him now, and I didn't know why, because I thought I had been seriously attracted to him. So I shook him off. And during the days after that, he'd show up at my office doorway and just stare. It looked like a snapshot of a stalker. And then he'd disappear, so I never knew when he was there and when he wasn't. It started to get spooky. I never knew if when I looked up he would be there, frozen and stiff, staring at me, or not. After that he didn't come into my office anymore. I found a box of stuff I'd left at his condo under my desk one day, but he must have left it there when I wasn't around. There was a couple pairs of panty hose and some make-up, my diet pills, my robe, and a couple of CDs.

The days that followed were stressful. I should have gone in to talk to him, but I couldn't stand to be near him. There was a company meeting with beers and hors d'oeuvres and the president got up to speak. When he spoke about the financial condition of the company, his eyes scanned all of the employees in the crowd. When they landed on me, just for a minute, there was a weird emotion on his face, but he was trying to hide it. He didn't let his eyes rest on me for too long.

When I got the e-mail from the human resources director, I knew what it was about. After I talked to her

I cleared my things out from my desk and took my plants and my pictures and packed them all in a scented box to take home with me. When I left I saw the president standing at the front desk, talking to the new receptionist. He saw me but he looked away and looked at her. He took the phone receiver from her, and he looked at her, and I could tell right then that he noticed her. The moron, the puke bag! It made me sick to think of what he'd done to me.

THE SURGEON'S REFRIGERATOR

On warm summer nights, the surgeon's refrigerator was raided with the stealth of crafty raccoons. The refrigerator sat in the carport in a corner by coils of dark green hose, garbage cans, and shelves housing cans of paint and motor oil. The raider of the refrigerator walked on marshmallows; the geese in the wet backyard voiced no complaint or reaction when the refrigerator was raided of beer, wine, strawberries, cheeses, chicken fat from patients which the surgeon never ate, Italian cookies from Mrs. Randazzo which the surgeon did, and countless baskets of green beans and zucchini from the gardens of the doctor's other patients who could not afford to pay.

Dr. Doisy had a housekeeper who came along after his wife died. She wore flowered dresses and nylon stockings that creased around her ankles, making them look even fatter than they actually were. He thought of her as an old lady even though she was only three or four years younger than he was. When she baked and cleaned she reminded him a little of his mother. The housekeeper's name was Mrs. Dunwidee, and in the evenings the doctor kept his eye on her, because she nourished her gout, obesity, and cardio-vascular quirks with meats, cheeses, and bakery sweets, and she liked her liquor, and her laid-back, honest granny face did not erase her humanity. The doctor knew that even good people could make large mistakes.

He sometimes found himself comparing his housekeeper to his wife, who would have been around the same age as Mrs. Dunwidee, but who never would have been so fat. The doctor's wife had been pleasantly round and soft, as females should be, but by no means obese. And she wouldn't have lost her sense of smell, as Mrs. Dunwidee had, to walk around reeking of perfume so strong as to be almost intolerable. His wife's hair would probably have been white, unlike Mrs. Dunwidee's dyed abomination of dark brown hair above seventy-year-old wrinkles, which revealed her as a foolish old woman in a sad attempt to recapture her youth.

Dr. Doisy sat in his little study in the evenings with his Rhine wine, reading his medical journals and sometimes reading Mark Twain, but actually listening intently for the rustle of Mrs. Dunwidee's fat stockinged thighs to reach the vicinity of the door to the carport, where the outdoor refrigerator was. The old lady often hummed, and to Dr. Doisy this was like a kind of vibration mechanism when matched with his keen ears; he liked a quiet house, and every burst of musical breath from Mrs. Dunwidee's nasal passages was to him like a bounce of radar to a bat. He kept the door of his little study cracked, but all he saw of her, normally, was a shadow, or part of her ample rear end as she passed his door to retire to her suite at the end of the house.

She wasn't quiet, and she had a tendency to alert the geese. This happened one night when he heard her making noise with paper bags in the kitchen, and then heard the squishing of the nylon thighs and the creaking of the door to the carport. The geese screamed and cackled from the back yard.

"Mrs. Dunwidee!" he called. There was no reply. The sound of a metal trash can falling came to him, and then the slamming of the door. "Mrs. Dunwidee!"

She appeared at his study doorway. She cautiously pushed open the door. Her brown eyes blinked at the light from the floor lamp by his chair. Crumbs graced her thin lips.

"What was that noise?" he said.

"I was takin' the trash out. I always take the trash out at night, but sometimes I forget. And then it's dark out there and I'm always knocking things over. You really should put a light out there. I could get raped."

The doctor stared at her for a moment, but elected to say nothing. He was going to say something about the refrigerator, but she interrupted him and he lost his train of thought.

"You know, Doctor," she said. "I have a problem with my knee. Here I am working for you, and I have ailments."

"What's the matter with your knee?" he said quietly. He hoped she would not be so modest as to refuse his taking a look at it.

"It's right here," she said. She propped her heavy foot, with the old lady shoe, up on his knee, and threw her skirt up so high on her thigh that the doctor was alarmed at first. Mrs. Dunwidee's leg was varicose blue. She pointed to her knee. "It's something in the joint," she said. "Only I don't think it's arthritis or bursitis or nothin' like that because it just got there yesterday."

"Did you fall, or bump it, or otherwise injure it, that you remember?" he said.

"Nah I didn't do nothing like that." She still stood on one leg with her other firmly and heavily planted on his knee. He could suddenly take it no more; he pushed her leg off, a little more roughly than he intended, and her shoe pounded the hardwood floor and threw her off balance for a moment. She brushed herself off as if she'd been in a fist fight. "Well that's not very doctorly," she said. "That's not bedside manner." Dr. Doisy went back to his reading

Long after Mrs. Dunwidee's light went out that evening,

the doctor sneaked to the refrigerator for a look. A six pack of Bud and a package of doughnuts were missing.

Dr. Doisy watched her one night. It disgusted him to think he was spying on Mrs. Dunwidee, but he tiptoed barefoot around the house none the less, peeking around corners and listening through doors. After she cleaned up the dinner dishes and pots and pans she wiped the counters with her fat yellow sponge. She went to her room and there were some questionable sounds from within, arousal sounds, to his imagination and dismay—and the doctor thought he smelled cigarette smoke, but he couldn't be sure. That's all Mrs. Dunwidee would need for her ailments!, the doctor thought, but he shoved the matter aside and went to his study to sit in the dark. He soon fell asleep, and when he woke he thought he had caught Mrs. Dunwidee in the act because he heard refrigerator sounds—jars clinking together, the crackling of plastic wrap. But she was only in the kitchen fixing a cup of tea and rummaging around for milk.

The next night he had planned on watching her but fell asleep in his chair early in the evening, reading about surgical techniques involving the gall bladder. He woke to the sound of the door to the carport slamming, and he was quickly on his bare feet, tiptoeing toward the kitchen.

What he saw revolted him. Mrs. Dunwidee wasn't even dressed. She came back into the kitchen with a flashlight wearing a gargantuan bra and a pair of underpants that covered her blubbery peaks and valleys only minimally; the underpants were huge and came up to her rib cage. The doctor had operated on the likes of her before, but the re-suturing through measures of fat was torture, and he did not like the sight of someone like this walking around his carport or his kitchen with a flashlight. He witnessed this through the crack of the swinging door to the dining room and the wall, and, to his horror, Mrs. Dunwidee's brown eye met his on the other side of the crack, only a few inches away, and winked! This frightened him considerably, and he went straight upstairs to his dark room to jump in his bed.

✦

"I've been wanting to ask you about the refrigerator," she said the next morning, a Saturday.

It bothered Dr. Doisy that he had to converse with the housekeeper while still in his bathrobe, but he could never wait for his coffee. He liked to have at least one cup before he showered and dressed. He felt his own expression brighten at the mention of the refrigerator. The secret would be revealed at last. "Fire away," he said.

"It seems to me that your eating habits have changed, Dr. Doisy," she said. "It seems to me like they say, 'Doctor heal yourself,' because you have been taking a lot of strange stuff out of that refrigerator outside, like cookies and beer at the same time, like the chicken fat in the jar that's been in there God only knows how long—what do you eat it with, crackers?"

"Mrs. Dunwidee, I promise you," he started, and then smiled. "I have not been into the outdoor refrigerator. As I told you months ago when you started here, that refrigerator is strictly for extras which have no place inside the house."

"Well somebody's been taking crap out of that refrigerator," she said. "Somebody's been sneaking crap out of there. Because stuff's there one minute and gone the next." She sniffed. "I have to hose down the carport on account of those geese coming in for the sack of corn—they know where the corn is, Doctor, you can't fool them—and I have to hose it down and squirt the green goose doo out, and I most always check that refrigerator, to see if we need anything."

Mrs. Dunwidee's blatant denial began to enrage the doctor. Her secrecy, as hired help, was bad enough; this blaming behavior was too revolting for words, so he said nothing.

She continued. "And so I notice when stuff's missing. And let me tell you, it's missing a lot these days. It's like some kind of weird ass food binge you're on." Her bovine eyes blinked and dared him to reply.

He took a sip of coffee and cleared his throat. "As I have said. I have nothing to do with the refrigerator in the carport. Excuse me while I take my coffee to my room!"

"You can't fool me, Doctor!" she shouted after him, but he was already halfway up the stairs.

✦

Dr. Doisy was a teaching doctor, or used to be, and this allowed him certain privileges with the university medical school, and he came home with the hand of a corpse one day to put in the refrigerator, to discourage Mrs. Dunwidee from her thievery, lies, and accusations. The severed hand included a wrist, but not much more, and it was a little blue around the edges. The rigor mortis of the hand prevented him from wrapping it around a three-liter bottle of Merlot that was in the forefront of the top shelf of the refrigerator, but he put it near, because whatever booze was there always disappeared first. It looked impressive. To the surgeon, who was used to seeing things like severed hands and other parts of corpses, the hand had little shock value, but he knew that Mrs. Dunwidee would feel differently; to those with little exposure to corpses, any part of them was an experience. He also placed an empty tuna can on the place where the refrigerator door met its body, to alert him when somebody opened the door. Then he went inside and washed his perpetually chapped hands.

For nights on end he waited. The big white geese made their nest and took turns sitting on it, adjusting their feathered bottoms to make themselves comfortable. They honked more than ever now for no apparent reason. He spied, but Mrs. Dunwidee never went out to the refrigerator. And then one day she went out, and he heard the can drop and the refrigerator door slam, and she came lumbering back in with a carton of milk which she put in the refrigerator in the kitchen, as cool as you please. It was very early in the morning and Mrs. Dunwidee had sleep seeds in her eyes, but the surgeon could not imagine that she'd missed seeing the hand, unless she'd accidentally put groceries in front of it, so he went out to check. In the gray of the morning, he opened the refrigerator door to find produce, cheeses, milk, Merlot, and the severed hand. Everything was there. When he closed the door and turned around, to his horror, Mrs. Dunwidee squinted at him from the kitchen door. The look was victorious.

"What have you done with my Merlot?" he cried.

"I haven't done nothing," she said. She still smiled. "I haven't done nothing and it's time you got out of these habits, Doctor, because I am beginning to think I am working for a lunatic!" And the fear that crossed her face at that moment caused the doctor to believe she might be serious, or at least that he owed her the benefit of the doubt.

"It's not like I don't eat any of your food or nothing. I eat what you provide, but I have to eat. And I have a drink now and then. But I sure don't ransack this refrigerator and take what I'm not supposed to take, and that is for sure!" Her eyes were round. They filled with tears, and her whole body began to quake. Although Dr. Doisy was a compassionate man, this was distasteful. Apparently she hadn't even noticed the hand—or had she? The whole situation baffled him. He replaced the tuna can and retired to his den to read *Only One Man Died: The Medical Aspects of the Lewis and Clark Expedition*.

✦

That night, just as he was getting to the parts about blood-letting, leeches, and a doctor named Benjamin, he heard a faint noise like a whisper from outside the house. Dr. Doisy rose quietly from his leather chair and padded through the kitchen in his thick wool socks. The kitchen was dark and large. He opened the door to the carport cautiously, hoping it wouldn't squeak on its hinges, but as he did so, a small figure in something like a oversized sport coat, like a miniscule stick man in loose rags, ran from the driveway into the moonlit honeysuckle vines beyond the house. The tuna can was still on top of the refrigerator. He'd interrupted the thief in time.

✦

The next morning, the Dean of the medical school rang Dr. Doisy's doorbell. Mrs Dunwidee answered. Dr. Doisy knew this young, hippie-type Dean; he was a man with a good reputation in medicine and in higher education, but he was young and naïve, and he didn't know much about Doisy's former position within the university, let alone his subsequent Chief of Surgery positions in hospitals. Dr. Doisy shivered in his four poster bed, none the less, to hear Mrs. Dunwidee talking to the man in a crude voice: "I don't know! The doctor isn't awake yet. He's an old man, you know. But I'll tell him, sir, yeah. I'll tell him when he wakes up."

Dr. Doisy had mixed feelings about Mrs. Dunwidee's calling him an old man. These passed quickly. The Dean may have gotten wind of the missing cadaver hand, but one couldn't be sure. The hippie could have been on a perfunctory visit. Dr. Doisy jumped out of bed like a jack-in-the-box to look out the window and see the ruffian upstart retreat from the house past the overflowing stone flower pots and the emerald rug lawn. Then the doctor entrenched his head in the mattress under the feather pillow. The Dean of the medical school faded into the background and disappeared, and Dr. Doisy fell back into his dreams: sexual dreams of his wife and Dickensian dreams of stinking illness, poverty, and righteousness.

The next night brought an authentic nightmare. After dining on Mrs. Dunwidee's salmon loaf and chilled green beans and retiring to the den, and after resuming the medical aspects of the Lewis and Clark expedition, Dr. Doisy heard the resonance of the tuna can—like percussion and horns at the same time. It was so loud, in fact, that it physically jarred him from his chair, and he was on his feet in a flash, running through the lit kitchen, in which Mrs. Dunwidee stood like the squiggle and dot of a question mark with a bottle of brandy, a barely drunken quandary on her face, in her gold furry slippers and obscenely flowered muumuu. This distracted him for a moment before he flew to the door to the carport, and he blamed the distraction for the lack of what he thought he saw at first: the refrigerator door was open, its interior forty-watt bulb throwing light on the tuna can that lay on the concrete floor. The refrigerator door remained open because it was propped that way by the trap door of the little freezer, a door which was normally glued and crusted shut by layers of frost and ice. A bag of frozen peas gaped open at the entrance to the freezer. Peas rolled out in twos and threes to bounce and roll on the floor of the carport, away from the light. Dr. Doisy followed a couple of these with his eyes, and as his eyes adjusted to the semi-darkness beyond the weak light, he saw a pair of sandals with feet inside. A small, skeletal girl of thirteen or so stood in the half light, staring at the open refrigerator in rage, her eyes watering and her mouth open. She wore a hobo-like tweed coat that was ten sizes too big for her. The legs of her jeans were frayed, filthy, and torn. Her hair was matted like an animal's and her face looked filthy, even in the half light. She looked up at him, swore at him, and ran away toward the woods where cicadas buzzed and a whippoorwill called with even, melodious cries. He heard her footsteps in the tangle of honeysuckle and leaves.

Dr. Doisy swept up the hard peas and threw them into the metal garbage can. He closed the bag of peas, secured the trap door of the freezer, and closed the refrigerator door. He stepped out of the carport and walked out to the edge of the driveway, straining to listen, but there was no crackling of sticks, no tripping over roots or vines, only the cicadas and the whippoorwill. The night was typically warm and humid, with the smell the strong scent of the yellow roses that lined his driveway.

"Dr. Doisy? What is going on out here?" Mrs. Dunwidee unsteadily emerged from the kitchen into the carport. "Are you out here? What happened out here?"

"Go on in and go on to bed now, Mrs. Dunwidee," he said. "Nothing happened. We can talk in the morning."

When he was sure she had gone to her room, he pulled a ziplock bag from a kitchen drawer, retrieved the hand from the refrigerator, and dropped it in. It landed palm-up. He put the ziplock into a trash bag and dumped the whole contraption into his metal garbage can. He replaced the tuna can on top of the refrigerator, returned to the kitchen to scrub his hands, and went back to the study with what was left of the bottle of brandy Mrs. Dunwidee had possession of earlier. He was unable to read.

For a good month, perhaps longer that summer, Dr. Doisy left food in the carport. He propped a board across a couple of saw horses, near the refrigerator, and on top of that he left roast chicken, grapes, salad, bread and butter, roast beef sandwiches. He accompanied these with milk and fruit juice drinks of various kinds. On one or two occasions, very late, he heard the geese cry out, but when he went to the carport to check, nothing was disturbed. On one night, he heard a fracas and checked, only to find a large stray mutt wolfing down a roast beef sandwich. He chased the dog away, surprising himself at the extent of his anger.

"A hungry little urchin" were the only words he used to Mrs. Dunwidee to explain himself, and he was very glad she accepted these without comment, but he had the uncanny feeling almost all of the time that she was watching him—through door cracks, around the corners of his house, even from behind bushes in the garden. He had become a little paranoid. He left the food, like a butler, on the board in the carport and went to his study to read or to wince as he thought about the hippie Dean, who only called one evening to say that he'd stopped by one day to express his regards.

Dr. Doisy read Dostoevsky, Turgenev, Thomas Mann, Margaret Mitchell, James Joyce, and countless, endless historical works in his study as he waited. The waiting demanded long novels, exhausting ones, or infinite explanations of history: *The History of Europe, The Complete Works of Winston Churchill, An Explanation of Africa.* He read until his eyes watered or until he fell asleep in his chair, still listening for a sound from the carport as he felt his head nod like a bird's. He waited, but she never came.

DOG LEG

Brutus had intense yellow eyes that locked onto yours when he looked at you and cocked his head, but his eyes were closed when he was on the operating table. Joe had the OR nurse cover him with blue sheets and only his feathery, mottled tail stuck out. Joe was operating on his leg.

Joe has always been smarter than me and now that he is a doctor he is a lot smarter. Or so I thought, until he did this thing with Brutus. I don't even know where he got Brutus. We are two typical brothers, very different, but that's okay. Joe has very delicate hands, like a girl's hands, soft and white. I am a sawman. I sell meat-cutting saws to butchers and grocery store chains and am missing a few fingers as a result.   Joe is a sawbones. We laugh about it.

Joe's wife found out that Joe was seeing this nurse. She suspected for a long time, and then she found out for sure. So he had to do something, so he bagged the little nurse and decided to fix up Brutus because Dobie loves Brutus. She probably loves him more than Joe, now.

Dobie is beautiful. I was there right after each one of her four kids was born and before I quit drinking we used to get drunk together. Or I got drunk. I live alone and so spend a lot of time at Joe and Dobie's. One time, we played with glow-in-the-dark cereal box toys in their big kitchen, Dobie and me, drinking beers. They were these glow-in-the-dark octopus things that you throw at the wall and they stick and walk down the wall in the dark with their octopus legs. We drank a bunch of beers and turned off all the lights and threw them at the walls and the cabinets and the refrigerator for hours. She is very beautiful.

Brutus used his three good legs as best he could when he ran around with the children in their spongy, green yard. He ran around trees and bushes and through leaves and even vaulted his ass over the snow in the wintertime with his one good leg, but sometimes he yelped. His bad leg was always a few inches off the ground, and he always smelled like the weather. He also had that clean soft smell that hunting dogs have, the ones with the soft fur with little spots. Brutus was a mutt, and it was evident he had some Brittany in him, and he had those penetrating, lock-on eyes that labs have, but he was scrawny and his head was shaped a little like a hound dog's head. So he looked ridiculous. But at the same time, when he looked at you, you could definitely tell somebody was in there.

✦

I hear them in the kitchen. Dobie is banging dishes and coffee cups around, throwing away trash. At first I can hardly hear them, then their voices get louder.

"I was there Joe," Dobie says. "I saw you."

"What did you see?" Joe says. "Me? Having lunch in the cafeteria with a nurse? So I'm not supposed to have a life?"

Dobie doesn't say anything.

I am sitting in the living room in an antique chair with the stuffing falling out and Brutus is there, standing on three legs with his bad one off the ground, as usual. He looks at me and blinks, then looks toward the kitchen. He looks at me again, then flops down and puts his head on his front paws, ears perked, quietly staring at the kitchen. He takes in a deep breath and lets it out all at once. I am sitting there with a magazine and the place smells like mothballs. The whole big house always smells like mothballs. Maybe they want to preserve all their antiques. They have lots of antiques and art, and rugs so pretty that you hate to walk on them.

Joe says, "Are you obsessed or something?" He swears.

"The subject is closed," says Dobie. I hear her cough. "I'm not going to talk about it any more. I just wanted to tell you that I know."

"Know what?" Joe knows he is caught, but he is scrambling. He is pulling out all the stops when it comes to his acting ability.

She doesn't say anything.

"Know what?"

Dobie knows he wants her to react so that he will have a chance to defend himself. He used to do that to me all the time when we were growing up and I recognize it. Dobie says nothing, and my brother knows he is a goner. He has been found out. No more nurse, and probably no more family as he knows it, because Dobie is not a dependent woman.

He swears again and it sounds like he throws something down on the kitchen table, a book or something. Then he comes in to the living room, looking dead. His face is gray and wet.

And then he sees Brutus, who wags his tail and smiles at Joe; you can see the half moons of the whites of Brutus' eyes on the bottom as he looks up, and all of a sudden Brutus is Joe's best friend. The truth is that at this point Brutus is probably Joe's only friend. He sure as hell is not my friend right now, and I do not want to call him my brother.

Joe smiles, color comes back to his face, and he quickly drops to his knees and cradles the mutt dramatically in his arms, which makes Brutus emanate starry-eyed happiness as if on a hallucinogenic high, because he is not used to this display of affection from Joe. For the rest of the night the dog limps around everywhere after Joe. Joe gives him words of encouragement occasionally, but does not speak to Dobie. He acts as if he is insulted. How dare she. The angrier he becomes with his wife for acknowledging the truth, the more attention he gives to the dog.

✦

I never knew how Joe talked two anesthesiologists into properly drugging the dog for surgery, or how they even knew the right dose for a dog like Brutus, or how he got them to keep quiet about the dog being in the hospital in the first place. I thought about this when they both administered the stuff through plastic tubing into the dog's body. One was a young guy and the other an older female. Their eyes were all smiles over their masks. If I saw them today I would not recognize them.

Joe gave Brutus some Librium and put him in the burlap bag before sneaking him through the back door of the Illinois hospital in the wee hours of a Wednesday morning. The Librium didn't exactly make Brutus go to sleep; it just made him dopey, and after he was in the bag you could picture his stoned hound dog head bouncing up and down in a state of stupefied confusion. Joe and I still had to negotiate some pretty long halls and get past some technicians of various ilks and persuasions; there are lots of people who work running machines in the hospital.

"Hi Doctor," they said, or "Hello, Doc." Joe looked straight ahead down a long hall and nodded, determined to get past them with the lumpy figure in the burlap bag. Nobody said anything about it.

Joe opened up Brutus' leg on the operating table. The operating room was all alcohol and needles, hoses and rubber, and it made me kind of sick. I didn't want to look at the inside of the dog leg but I got the idea of what Joe was doing when he picked up a small metal rod from his array of instruments and paraphernalia and attached it there on the inside of Brutus. Joe had this fixed, angry expression on his face, almost like he hated Brutus. His eyes were bulging and the skin around his mask was red and sweaty. He needed a shave, and his effeminate, white hands were shaking. Brutus was then the proud owner of a pin in his leg, the way people have pins in their hips or knees or the like. Joe was trying to compensate for some congenital screw-up that made Brutus' leg bent and useless, and he used the pin to straighten it out.   Then he sewed Brutus back together like a stuffed animal and we cleaned up, which left a little time for the anesthesiologists to keep an eye on him.

✦

He came out of the anesthesia a little earlier than he was supposed to. This caused a problem on the way out of the hospital, when I was behind Joe in a long hall and the bag started wiggling a little. The movement got stronger as we rounded a corner, and there was a nun there who wanted to talk to Joe, and right about then the bag started whipping back and forth. Brutus was awake and trying like hell to get out of the bag.

"What do you have there, Doctor?" the nun said. She had glasses that magnified her brown eyes, and a modern nun habit.

I knew Joe was sweating it. He could have been kicked off the staff of the hospital for sneaking Brutus in for surgery like that. The bag was twisting and whipping and Brutus was kicking with what must have been his good leg, unless Joe's handiwork had worked instantly. You could see the hound dog head shape pushing on one side of the bag trying to get out.

Joe didn't reply to the nun. He looked alarmed and walked away. I looked at the nun and shrugged, and she was staring at him as he walked away with the flailing bag.

I could feel the nun observing us even when we were nearing the door. She was wearing those quiet shoes nuns and nurses wear, but you could tell she was there.

Right about then Brutus lost control of his bowels. What looked like a bucketful of brown liquid came right through the burlap bag with a rush and hit the floor with a sound like when somebody puked in grade school.

The look on the nun's face was pretty much what you'd expect, but Joe's face was something to see, because in addition to his terror at being found out he slipped a little bit on the stuff on the floor and had to regain his balance. He mouthed a few swear words and sweated bullets, holding tight to the bag. Then he ran down the hall, took a right down another long hall and I ran after him, past all those people who worked the machines in the hospital again, who were jerking their heads around to stare, and out the door he went with me after him.

✦

One night when I stopped by Dobie was alone and very drunk. She'd polished off half a jug of wine. She was sitting on the floor in the kitchen in the middle of pieces and splinters of broken china and glass when I walked in. Brutus was sitting next to her. I don't know where the kids were. I thought they were there at first because I heard her talking to someone when I came near the kitchen.

"And we will find out," she was saying. "We will find out everything. When he started it, how he started it, what happened exactly, and I mean exactly. How can we do it?"

I saw her when I rounded the corner of the kitchen. Her eyes were puffy and I noticed the gray streaks in her red hair for the first time. She was old and pathetic, sitting there on the floor with her veiny legs splayed, and I don't know how but she became even more beautiful to me then. She was looking at Brutus, who was who was smiling up at her with his half moon eyes and half-wagging, and she was nodding in agreement to nothing.

"Yes, we can take that *additude*," she said. She had trouble saying it. Then she noticed me. She was not at all startled.

She petted the dog, and then tried to wink at him. "We'll get to it later," she said to him in a drunk-loud whisper. And then to me in a regular voice, "Well John. You are just in time to help me clean this shit up. Sometimes I get tired of being the only one to do the dishes."

There was some fruit in the next room, the dining room. A peach had exploded where it made contact with a wall. She must have hurled it in there, because the fruit bowl that she kept on the table in the kitchen was on its side in the hall. I picked some of it up and went back to the kitchen to get something to clean up the wall.

"Where's Joe?" I said.

Instead of answering, she stood up and stared at Brutus, eyes wide, and he smiled and half-wagged in anticipation of whatever it was she was about to do or say. "Brutus!" she said. "Did you hear that?"

Then she turned to me and said, "We were just wondering the same thing. We think we know, *roughly*." When she said roughly, a spray of spittle came from her mouth to my shirt like a garden mister, very fine. I must have looked alarmed, because she put her hand on my arm. "Don't worry," she said. "Brutus is here, and he understands! He understands everything! All you need to do is look at him, and he knows! It must be some kind of telepathy! And he cares!" She looked down at him with tears in her eyes and he kind of stood at attention, very obedient.

✦

Joe buried Brutus in the same burlap bag he had hauled him out of the hospital in, past the nun. The body was limp, and nothing came out. I went out to the back with Joe, with the dog corpse in the bag, and Joe didn't say much. The dog's leg had gotten infected before he had gotten a chance to use it very much, and the infection had killed him.

Dobie watched him dig a hole and put the dog body in it, and I watched too. There was something crazy in his eyes and on his face as he dug, he bit his lip with every stroke of the shovel and eventually it bled, and he was dripping with sweat before he was through.

It's funny how life goes though, how the nurse thing led to blood and sweat and burying Brutus and Dobie's not being Joe's wife anymore. I could tell that by looking at her that day. Joe had trashed their friendship and buried Brutus all in the same year and from this day forward Dobie would be a million miles away from him, and she was lonely and confused and very cold.

I waited until I could catch her eye there at the sliding glass door. She was looking past me, past Joe, toward the woods in back of him. I smiled and waved at her and hoped that she would do the same.

Robbie Rockett sells furniture in a blue collar neighborhood in south St. Louis where everything is sold in sets. The store tries to appeal to the suburban market and that's why Robbie, an adolescent creature of the suburbs, was hired. When he got the job in the city he told everyone there to call him Bob, but a high school classmate came in with his mother to look at a sofa and referred to him as Robbie, so everyone in the store did likewise. His cards say "Bob Rockett, Fine Furniture Specialist" is raised red letters.

Robbie loves the store in the morning, when the sun shines at just the right angle through dirty windows, making a cloudy and surreal environment for large painted ceramic dogs, vulgar floral overstuffed sofas, Queen Anne chairs and dusty gold mirrors. Silk flower centerpieces on early American coffee tables, almost alive. He enters his yellow cloud of tangible things, shutting out the toothless and tattooed of that part of the city.

Robbie turns on the overhead lights in the display cases and china cabinets, taking time to preen before their mirrored backgrounds of beveled glass. He feels his adolescent beard stubble, picks at a tooth.

Back before he tried to escape his name, Judith fell in love with Robbie Rockett. She was thirteen when he spotted her at a high school football game. Robbie was infatuated with the school's Pep Club president, Vicki Halloren. Vicki was crowned Prom Queen and Robbie Rockett adored her. He followed her, spied on her, befriended her dates (to their bewilderment) and joined her causes. He revved the engine of his purple Mercury when she was in sight. And all of this he did with a hard-on. Every time. Judith noticed this.

✦

Judith lies on her back on a Thomasville sofa in the furniture store at 2:00 a.m. on a Saturday morning, legs apart and shaking, waiting for the insertion of Robbie Rockett's penis. (Sex education: the penis is always inserted into the vagina. Not crammed, rammed or pushed.) Her head is full of bourbon and Robbie Rockett is excited. He has never done this before, and she has never done this before, which is what excites him, because he read and heard it was supposed to be exciting.

✦

"Guide it in! Goddam, put it in!" he says.

Judith is not sexually excited, even though she adores Robbie Rockett, treasures him. At fourteen, she wants to study to be a veterinarian; pictures herself operating on animals with Robbie Rockett as her husband.

Robbie's penis is the strangest thing she has ever seen. It is like chicken gristle, slightly elastic, and moves in jerks. It looks ancient, as if it has been attached to Robbie Rockett for many lifetimes.

"Don't laugh, goddam it! Put it in!" Robbie's face is a red carnation with emerald eyes. His jug ears are the rosiest of all. He doesn't even seem to be enjoying himself. She realizes that this particular perception may revolt her later.

"Birds do it," she says. "Dogs do it. It looks easier for them."

Robbie shoves.

There were a few other times, on sweet suburban lawns or in damp basements. As before, Judith felt nothing but dull pain and a filled-up feeling. The first time had hurt; it seemed to her that the whole thing was entirely over-rated. At first she had enjoyed the affection but after a time Robbie wouldn't even kiss her anymore.

Then he didn't want to see her anymore.

✦

At her apartment complex, a communal balcony over-looks a wooded area; the summer air is heavy with humidity and it is hard to breathe. She is twenty-five and barely a veterinarian and it is a locust year. The insects hum madly in and around the trees. They crawl and drop on the hot balcony and she tiptoes around their exoskele-tal, triangular bodies. She bumps into an oversized chaise longue where two men are sleeping in the sun, arm-in-arm, wearing cutoffs. The man closest to her wakes, his eyelids open languidly and she is peering suddenly into the emerald eyes of Robbie Rockett. She says nothing, walks back inside and up the stairs to her apartment. On the way she glances back and sees his wiry posture sitting up before a background of dropping bugs.

✦

Ordinarily, she thinks, the old women in the grocery store in her suburban town, who lean on their carts to chat, having taken leave of their cautious steps, talk about the weather or the priest or the crap on the local TV news. Yet this is how she learns that Robbie Rockett is sick. The baggy-ankled women who pretend that their legs were never apart—in the midst of dozens of children and grandchildren—are having a heyday of a grocery trip. One of them smells bad and has whiskers.

Robbie Rockett is dying at his mother's house.

Judith goes through life with her husband and her children and her examinations of animals thinking about this, about what he did to her, his blatant infatuation with the Prom Queen and his ultimate, blissful comfort with the man on the balcony, in the company of locusts.

Sometimes, when she is having sex with her husband primarily for his purposes, she finds herself frigid and shivering in the furniture store, glaring at a ceramic Dalmatian or pondering a silk flower centerpiece which sells for $49.95.

✦

He lies under a smooth sheet and a white, bumpy bedspread with fringe, propped up by immense pillows. The room is bright, but the size of the pillows suggests a hospital though he is at his mother's home.

He lies there, no more than a stick with a skull head, bald, static electricity lifting the hairs on his arms like the legs on a hairy spider. Doesn't even move his head very much. It looks as if he is already dead, there are so many red flowers in the room; acrid red carnations. The bony toes of his right foot are exposed beyond the fringe of the bedspread, with their own plumes of spider hairs. Amazingly enough, as pale as he is, she notices that his jug ears are slightly pink, as they were twenty years ago.

He rolls his eyes in her direction as she enters the room. Doesn't turn his head. It must hurt him, she thinks.

When it sinks in, when he realizes who she is, he turns his head fully in her direction and his mouth opens slightly.

She sits on a chair by the bed. "So," she says.

"What did you get yourself into this time?"

"Very funny," he says. His voice still has the young and

fresh quality that it had when he was seventeen.

Out of that bald, skull head.

"Aren't you glad I came to see you?" she says. "I mean, hasn't your life flashed in front of your eyes, like a kind of Robbie Rockett video—at least a few times by now?"

"My name is Bob," he says.

She lights a cig. "Okay. A Bob Rockett video. Doesn't it contain fleeting moments in the furniture store, flashes of Vicki Halloren wearing a crown—a crown!—of your parents, but most importantly," she puffs. "Most importantly, I should think, highlighted should be when you lost your virginity!" She laughs quietly and coughs.

Robbie Rockett starts to smile. "Was it good for you?"

"No," she says, just before she understands that this is his sarcastic attempt at being kind.

A look of alarm crosses his face then, and he goes into a kind of spasm. Judith looks on, intrigued.

The skull head shudders and bounces. She rests her chin on her hands, her elbows on her knees, and squints. His eyes almost close as he shudders and his body stills itself as he dies.

Ironically, he wears the same half smile in his new state that accompanied his last question. It reminds her of a character from *Wind In the Willows,* but she cannot remember which one.

"I'm sorry," she says. "I thought you were someone else."

She clasps his hands together on his chest to form the classic corpse and embellishes them with red flower buds snapped from their stalks. She does not look back at him again before she leaves the house.

THE TUTOR

The math tutor had a wife, but he didn't know how to love her.

This is how I learn about math.

He is waiting for me in his little room. It must be eighty-five degrees in there and still he wears a blanket over his lap; the Catskills are covered with a light snow and the wind is blowing fiercely. The weather makes the whole experience all the more eerie because I am being dropped off by my mother—abandoned in the snow— at the rickety white farmhouse and the stinking old guy with his blanket who is inside. He is supposed to teach me algebra. There are a couple of pigs outside.

I was never good at math and Mother blames society since I am a girl. It is an old argument and I am tired of it; math of any kind has never interested me, with the possible exception of making change. My fifth grade math teacher was a little wrinkled woman with bleached blonde hair that was teased on the top of her head, who looked and walked like an emperor penguin. She wore black and was very compact, except for her upper arms, and beyond a doubt the most interesting aspect of the class was when she passed out assignments or tests, toddling around the classroom in her little low-heeled black shoes. It must have been around this time that my math grades began to drop. The penguin/teacher combination intrigued me; I was not at all interested in New Math.

✦

Now," he says. He points to a simple algebraic equation in the book. "Now." He clears his throat, not very well. "Let's see what you know." His finger is yellowed, with a long nail. It looks like a piece of petrified wood. He runs his finger back and forth under the equation and I stare at it and he stares at it too.

"If A is less than B, and B is less than C, then A is less than C," I reply. "I think that's the property of transitivity." I squint at it because I'm really not sure, but it sounds logical.

There is a bottle of blackberry brandy and a glass half-full next to the book and the tutor exhales the nauseous, sweet smell of disease, of that sweet taste of flu congestion or the predecessor of puke, mixed with medicine and decay. "Right," he says.

Margaret Zinzelmeyer tiptoes into the room with a tray. She smiles radiantly with round sapphire eyes; her wrinkled face is still round and she has dimples. She is an old woman with dimples.

"I brought you your brandy Malcolm," she says. She brings in smells of baking spices and moth balls when she comes, and wears stockings with seams on her plump and squeezy calves. She carefully places another half-filled crystal glass to one side of him on the card table.

He waves her away. "Bring another bottle," he says in distaste.

She smiles hopefully. "And would the little pupil like some apple bread?" she asks.

"Get out of here!" the tutor says.

She pats his bald head very softly, twice, and vanishes.

He frowns at the table and opens my algebra book, and then he looks at me directly. His milky eyes are magnified to golf ball circumference behind his glasses. "Life is a shit sandwich, and every day I take another bite!" he whispers. He blinks. "Now. Let's move on to positive and negative numbers."

✦

The math tutor and I play Yahtzee and dominoes far more than we study algebra. Most of the time we play Yahtzee. The tutor likes to roll the dice. I love the sound they make in the little brown, felt-lined cups, which still smell new. The tutor throws them overhand and they fall off of the table a lot, and he makes me crawl around on the oak floor to read them and tell him what he rolled. There is a rug on the floor; one of those that looks like a rope in an oval spiral and often smells like a dog. This one smells like a dog, too, but there is no dog anywhere around.

Before making any game decisions, the tutor takes his time, all the more interminable because of the emphasis added by the tic-tic-tic clock in his room. He takes a couple of belts of sherry and says "ahhh," after each, and says "now let me see." Then he breathes heavily through his hairy nose, which may have a whistle in it, and finally makes his move. After that he nods off like a bird, his head bob, bob, bobbing before hitting his chest. After he passes out I practice my rolls or line up the dominoes on the card table around his bony hands and knock them down.

I hear the grinding of our station wagon tires on the snow and gravel outside and the tutor's wife comes in to tell me that it's time to leave. She pats her husband on the head before she follows me out of the room.

✦

Once, when the tutor is asleep, and his wife has left the house to feed the pigs, I creep up the wood stairs, all the way up to the attic. From the attic window I see her flowered farm-wife dress blowing up against her legs and somehow this looks indecent; she is at other times so gracious and composed. She throws garbage in the pig trough and they come trotting up on stiff pig legs.

There are framed photos in the attic, thrown in a corner. It smells like a barn attic even though it is a house attic, of timothy and rope. For a moment I am transfixed by a photo of the math tutor and his wife as I breathe the dusty farmhouse attic smell.

They are standing in front of this farmhouse, all dressed up and I wouldn't have recognized the tutor, but he was bald even then and in the photo he has the same eyes, except in the photo they are smiling. His wife is easily recognizable. Her dimples are genuine and deep as she gazes up at him in adoration and with a bit of humor, as if she has just whispered something sexual or secret to him. He faces the camera with obvious pride and with a bit of a reaction to whatever it was she just said, with a look of disbelief and appreciation at the same time. This is what I imagine, anyway. She owns the classic shapely figure of a female of her time. The photo is black and white, of course, but her hair looks as if it might have been strawberry blonde. It's white now.

I look out the window again to see her heading back to the house, squinting against the blowing snow and barnyard dust. For a moment she gazes up at the house as if she knows I'm watching and the blue eyes twinkle all the way up to the attic. I descend the stairs then to wake the tutor and resume my algebra lesson.

✦

"If A equals B, then B equals A. Reflexive property," I say. "Good," breathes the tutor.

He pays no attention to his wife. She appears with a hopeful expression each day I am there, and since

I have seen the photo I assume it is because she wants to recapture the past. She wants to whisper something humorously obscene in his ear and elicit at least a smile, if not more. She comes, she goes. She does whatever it is he wants her to do.

The repetition: the clock, the stink, the tutor, his wife, the numbers and small letters that are algebra and that make little sense to me. His finger moving back and forth under an equation. His wife patting his head before she goes. It is unbearable.

◆

I show up and he is sitting with his back to the door to his room, as usual; his bald, veined head is bent forward toward the table. I can just barely see the corner of the Yahtzee box past his body on the right side. The algebra book must be open to page seventy-nine in front of him. In my terror I know which page it is; I have not looked at it since my last visit with him and he is destined to know once we get going.

The smells of medicine, piss, smoke, old blankets, the ghost-dog rug and brandy greet me and heighten the terror. The time is near.

Yet the time of reckoning never comes, because the math tutor is not alive.

I don't figure out he is dead until I have taken my seat at the table and waited, respectfully, for a few minutes. He head remains bowed and at first I think he is reading or contemplating the algebra book. Yet the book is not open; the Yahtzee dice are still in their cups in the box. The skin on his face, particularly around his eyes, is a pure, white-blue. So he is dead. I have not seen a dead body before, but the tutor's body is obviously vacant.

There's a faint creaking of hardwood floors outside the door, growing louder. It is the tutor's wife bringing the bottle and glass! I stare at the Yahtzee box and take a couple of deep breaths—I do not want to see her reaction when she finds her husband is gone. If there were another door I would run out of it and walk home, and I even consider crashing through a window to escape witnessing the destruction of a religious philosophy, a life perspective of duty, this disparate love. If he doesn't yell at her, then surely she will know he is dead! And then what will she do?

If only she refrains from patting his head this time. If she pats his head she will feel how cold it is.

"I brought you your brandy, Malcolm!" she says. She looks brighter today; she has applied a little make-up and a floral perfume.

"And cookies for you!" she says to me. "No matter what he says." She puts down the bottle and glass, still at his back, and slides the cookies over to me. They are set on a lace doily on a flowered china plate.

But oh, God, then she pats his head, one-two, and walks out the door. As she is closing it the corpse's head lolls to the right and rests on what had been the tutor's shoulder, and his glasses fall off and land on the card table.

✦

Tic . . . tic . . . tic. I practice my rolls in an overhand fashion, the way the tutor used to do. I have placed his hand around his brandy glass and filled the glass to the top.

When the station wagon tires make their grinding and crushing sound up into the driveway I grab my book and run out of the front door, making sure I don't encounter the tutor's wife on the way out.

I don't want to look at her.

I needn't have worried, though. Mother and I pass her, a couple of miles down the road, toward town. She is bundled in a long brown coat and has wrapped a red paisley scarf around her head and tied it under her chin; wisps of white hair stick out from underneath it and frame her face, star-like. She hobbles in little brown boots and she is carrying a battered suitcase. She lowers her head and looks away as we drive by.

Now I can use a matrix to represent a system of equations, and using a coefficient I can convert it into triangular form. In turn I write other equations, from the bottom up, and substitute known values as before.

LOST CONGREGATION

Nevertheless, as we have mentioned already,
Mr. Golyadkin was buoyed up with the most confident hopes,
Feeling as though he had risen from the dead.

— Fyodor Dosteovsky, *The Double*

Chet waited for the oboe notes to pulse from the worn floorboards of the porch like the constant heartbeat in the Poe story, the "Telltale Heart" of Lois. Chet was both afraid and elated at the sound. After Lois died, he had deposited her earthly belongings—her glass beads, diamond ring, soft-mothball scented woolen things, and her oboe—in a trunk like a gypsy. With ceremony, he had ripped up floorboards of the porch with a claw hammer and dropped the trunk into a cavern of dirt and sand. He felt ambiguous when he heard the oboe. Lois sometimes seemed to prefer the playing of the oboe to making love to him.

He looked across the road in front of the house to the hollow-straw field where he had dumped fistfuls of Lois's ashes. Geordie, his sheltie, came out of the dog door with a clicking of toenails and barked stringy phlegm. The oboe notes didn't resonate from the cow pasture, from the remainder of Lois' body; the melodies came from below the floorboards, where her instrument was. This evening he rocked in his chair on the porch boards, drank a little whiskey, leaked a little urine, and watched determined calves leap over ravines after their mothers. Crickets began their wing-rubbing song when the sun went down over the oaks. Yet it was on this particular evening that he first saw himself walking down the road, like a renaissance. It was the himself of pre-mortem Lois, when he walked happily in rhythm, his shoulders bent back, wide like the proud scarecrow's, when he remembered how to shave at least every other day, and when he had clean underwear and an unsoiled handkerchief in his pocket.

"Hey!" he called. The figure waved and walked on. It disappeared around a bend of locust trees with honey-fragrant fringe. He surmised that the double might be going to the church, as he and Lois used to do, to sit in waxed pews and listen to rising voices.

Chet remembered when Lois sat with her legs dangling from the cracking wicker chair on the porch, her tubular arms crossed over her chest. "They didn't have to take my tits," she said.

Chester had never heard Lois use that term. "It's no big deal."

"It will be, when you take me to bed. It'll be like going to bed with a man." Chet had watched her stare at a resident lizard that had scratched up onto the porch. Its occluded eyes swept in all directions. The brown lizards lived in thin caverns in the rocks and grasses surrounding the house. Lois had grabbed a broom that was leaned up against the porch railing; she'd hacked at the lizard until it catapulted into blue air. The force of the broom bristles had severed most of its tail from the rest of its body so that the bulk of the lizard landed with a soft thump on the dirt. Its severed tail had wriggled, a tiny protesting snake, at Chester's feet. This was one of his last clear memories of Lois.

A few days later, again at dusk, Chester watched himself walk down the road. This time he wore a shirt stiff as

cardboard, a bow tie, and red suspenders. He held a bou-
quet of Sweet William, no doubt for his love. The double whistled what sounded like a classical tune. It jumped
over something on the road, and Chet wanted to follow
it, but he stayed put in fascination. He drank from a pint
of Ten High, dribbled a little urine, and finally stepped
onto eroded rugs in the house on his way to the bathroom. When he came out, Sonny waited in a ripped wing
chair in the living room. Sonny patted the dog.

"Sonny, want a drink?" said Chet.

"No."

"Some food?"

"No. You probably don't even have any food."

"Probably not much, no." Chet scratched his scalp.

Sonny wrinkled his eyes and forehead the way he always did before he said something he considered witty.
"You want to jump off a cliff or something? It could give
you a sense of reality."

Since Chet had seen this coming, he easily brushed it
aside. "Hey, you know what? I'm thinking about building
a monument to your mother."

"What kind of monument? A statue or something?"

"An altar." Chet went to the fly-egg kitchen and came
back with books about creative construction. The dog
toenails clicked behind him as he went, first on the wood
floor, then the linoleum, then the wood floor again. The
books were filled with four-color photographs of rock
and flower.

Sonny didn't look at them. "I was thinking you could stay
with me and Angie for a few days."

"What for?"

Sonny took a sudden interest in the books. "Just a visit."

"You planning on trapping me there?" Chet accused.
"Trapping me there then putting me away somewhere?
Well screw you, son." He sneezed from the accumula-

tion of dust in the house and watched a weed-like spider climb one of the curtains.

Sonny paused to clop together one of the books with an echoing alto noise. "It was only an invitation. You have to get out of here some time. You can't just sit around here and pick your nose and piss in your chair."

Watching Sonny was a little like watching his Other Self walk down the road. Sonny resembled Chet in gesture and mannerism—he rubbed his fingers together and twisted his thin lips and spoke with certain emphases—and his eyes were the same as Chet's. For a moment, Chet was caught up in the beauty of his willful son, and when he ruminated as to how Sonny also mirrored Lois—his ears, hand, his large and noble nose—he began to see a hazy aura build itself around Sonny's head and body, there where Sonny sat in the purple wing chair.

"Forget it," Sonny said. He tossed the altar-building books onto the dirty coffee table and left laboriously, giving the screen door a snap on the way out.

"Sure you wouldn't like to stay for dinner?" Chet called after him.

✦

Chet looked at the monthly church newsletter and sniffed its crisp and inky pages. He used to smell the onion skin of old bibles and hymnals too; there was something so comforting in this. Chet had not been to church in a long time, not since the little memorial service had taken shape after Lois passed on, when the parishioners launched spacecraft balloons. There was no reason to go. He still received the newsletter in his leaning mailbox each month, but it appeared as if the church had changed. Instead of the causes he and Lois had enjoyed investigating and working on—the battered women's shelter, the building and repainting of low income housing near Clear Creek—the church rag only printed things like "Invite Jesus to Your Dinner Table!" or "Have a Family Night!" or other things equally insulting to his intelligence and spirit. When Lois passed on into the Other Places, the church newsletter changed.

This was a conspiracy. There was no doubt. The church itself was a medium sized stone structure with pine trees around. Chet would not have been surprised if the very trees had vanished upon Lois' passing on. Church women had brought him slimy casseroles and pies on a couple of weekends following the memorial service, but he sensed an alternative mission in them: with their pious sighs and artificial sympathy (because no one knew what this loss was like), they seemed to be saying that they were only glad it hadn't happened to them. People had personal agendas. Upon thinking about it now though, Chet wondered if he shouldn't be included and involved again, if only for the memory of Lois. Sonny never went to church, but he was probably at the root of the conspiracy, none the less, on account of the stunt he tried to pull in inviting Chet to his house for a "visit." So Chet crabbed down the road to the church one morning, preferring to walk rather than to take the Ford truck. He half expected to see his Other Self walking down the road in front of him, but it was not to be.

The people at church did not know him. It had been some years since he'd been there, but the stubby and paranoid Harriet Bertram, the weird Walter Higgins who lived with ferrets, and the others—they all gaped an expression of feigned concern and curiosity. They did not ask him to stay for coffee. They did not mention a study group the way they did when he and Lois whispered, prayed, and connived with them years ago in the cold narthex. By far the most amazing difference in the group was that the new minister was Simon Bone, greasy-haired

Bone, who'd made passes at Lois in the middle of the Nelson Mandela get-out-of-jail celebration many years ago. Simon had somehow become minister within a span of five years! Simon had repeatedly pinched Lois' butt by the film projector that outlined Mandela's life and legacy, had sulked in the back pews, and had manipulated the former minister with money and gossip about who was shafting whom, who had whomever by the short-hairs, and etcetera. He had padded around the church behind all kinds of people in his pursuit of power. He had finally achieved it.

"Do you . . . do you not have Bible study groups now, like the Old Testament ones with the rabbis and everything?" Chet asked Simon.

"There's a family values group going on now," Simon said. "I'm sure they'd love it if you stepped in. You've been gone for a long time." Simon said it like an accusation, most likely in case Chet knew of Simon's habit of pinching Lois' butt. Chet did not cave in to this ridicule. He pumped Simon's gooey hand and got on his way home. Traversing the gravel, he read his church bulletin. A party was to take place at Simon's house over the coming weekend for his birthday. Chet's step quickened. Simon lived in the minister's house by the church! Simon had been such a bad dream as minister that Chet didn't think of it sooner. A remote raccoon dusted itself across the road ahead, a reminder to think positively and purely; perhaps Simon had studied life and learned a few things; maybe Simon was no longer that bad. Chet could take the truck into town and buy some new clothes: some shoes, trousers, and a shirt. As he made these plans he got sight of his Other Self ahead of him on the road, and the self walked zombie like, tottering from leg to leg, but otherwise looked as well groomed and dressed as it had the last time Chet had seen it—even better, because the Self had gotten a hair trim. The wind shifted to pepper Chet's nostrils with the masculine deodorant of his Other Self, although the apparition didn't wave to Chet this time.

The party held so many possibilities. He could rent a car! There were so many plans involved that Chet wondered if he had a sharpened pencil or a respectable pen in the tangled drawers of the farmhouse. He couldn't remember. But this was important, and he worried that he'd have to go into town just for a pencil or a pen. Then, too, he should continue real work on the altar for Lois. So far, he'd only dug into the ground a little to provide a nest for its foundation. He planned to use materials that represented Lois and the years he had spent in her care: oak branches, wildflowers, sandstone perhaps.

Chet staggered into the pantry. He had knocked a dusty hole in the wall there and placed a box inside in which he kept his money. The bank was not to be trusted because the bank once tried to rip off Lois. Lois had been summarily ripped off and charged all kinds of fees for checks that had not bounced. He reached into the hole and fisted a wad of chalky bills.

The rental car was an old Lincoln that smelled like a dirty ashtray. Chet liked leaning back in the seat and rotating the big steering wheel with an arc of his arm. The radio played Frank Sinatra, and Chet hated the sound of that, but it seemed to go along with the Lincoln. The wind kicked up. It smelled like rain, and Chet wore a tuxedo.

Simon Bone's house was just as he had imagined. It reclined among a shroud of oaks and hickories; a gravel-dirt driveway snaked up to it—a two-story with abnormally gold lights. Clouds crossed the moon when Chet got out of the car, and a wet fog embraced him from all corners. A goat gave a sickening bellow from the dark beyond the house. Chet trembled when he looked at the front door. He walked around to the side of the house, where a small porch loomed off of what looked like a windowed kitchen door to the outside. He climbed the steps to the porch and peered in. Simon Bone's house radiated candle light and the banter of society. A woman near his age, wearing a dark and medieval looking hat, fingered dollar sandwiches on a tray with a trembling hand; the other hand cupped a large wine glass filled halfway with blood-red wine. The men were of various ages and shapes, all northern and white. Most wore casual slacks. Chet shuddered at the thought of his rented tuxedo.

As if seeing his own reflection then, he looked at his Other Self on the other side of the glass. The Other Chet waved at him heartily and smiled. He opened the kitchen door. It had begun to rain.

"Come in, come in!" the other Chet said. He wore a fine red cashmere sweater and held a mug of beer. He gestured to a large woman in a blue dress who was playing corny tunes on an upright piano. "Happy birthday to the Reverend Bone!" he said.

"I'll tell you about bones," Chet said, not knowing what else to say. "Do you know about the effects of cremation? Do you know what's left, and how heavy it is?"

The Other Chet didn't reply. He watched Chet with empty eyes. Then he said: "Did you bring a present for Reverend Bone?" Chet could have brought something like dog shit for Bone, an elusive present which would have ignited the congregation into something like thought or study or rapture. But this was something Chet had forgotten, and he was deeply ashamed in the long run. His tuxedo felt stiff. "I'm a man without much means these days," he replied.

"Well! We can all understand that!" the Other Chet said, and he danced off to a dark hall.

The woman with the large butt and blue dress began

playing "You're a Grand Old Flag," and guests howled in unison. Cold blasts of rain sprinkled through open windows, but inside it was soggy and hot, all sweat, putrid breath, and ancient perfume. Simon himself stood in front of the fireplace, arms out and palms upturned like an icon. At that moment, Chester hated Illinois. He hated his empty farm, his pregnant cows, the dinner-plate moon. What had become of this place? What had become of his church? Big-butt at the piano, the fake eyelashed and girdled playgirls at this party were the very indicators of a change he did not want to imagine. The men used hairspray, he could tell.

Simon Bone tugged at his tux sleeve. "Glad you could come, Chet. We've all missed you."

This seemed like a genuine gesture, and Chet thought for a moment that he might reconsider the character of Simon Bone. Despicable or not, Bone was a man of the cloth. "Tell me, Simon," he said. "There is something I have to ask you, but I'm afraid of what you'd think."

"What?" said Bone. He was all beady eyes.

"There's a man here, and he looks to be an awful lot like me."

"There is? Wait. Yes, you mean the other Chester. Yes. There is. He looks like you and his name is the same. How odd!"

"So it wasn't just me? My imagination? Because I have one, Lord knows."

Simon fixed his whole being on Chet through the mechanism of his mouse eyes. "No, no, I don't think it's your imagination. There is a resemblance. But that can happen. Coincidence, God, who knows these things? It happens." Simon placed a pastoral hand on Chet's back. It felt heavy in the wood paneled hall, and for a minute Chet thought he might fall over. The weight of Bone's hand was overwhelming. At this point, a boy of eight or nine walked by in a sweater just like Simon's. He farted and stuck out his tongue at both of them. A woman with bleached hair, dark at the roots, followed him carrying a sexless baby that wallowed over the shoulder of her polyester dress. Simon Bone disappeared into what had become a mass of homogenous people. Chet helped himself to a glass of red wine. He gulped it fast and headed for the bathroom. The bathroom was tiny tiled; it had to accommodate a toilet and cracked pedestal lav and a shower with a shower curtain, and when Chet had finished his pee and turned around, the Other Chester bashed the new-plastic smelling shower curtain from the inside of the tub at him like an animal. "Booooo!" he shouted, and Chet ran from the room into the hot and filthy sweat of strangers who were, supposedly, part of Chet's forgotten congregation.

Harriet Bertram banged around the hardwood floors of Simon Bone's house with a walker and pretended not to know Chet until he addressed her directly: "Harriet, when did you find the need for that thing?"

"After I fell and broke my hip," Harriet said. "You really should be a little more sensitive, Chester. I have always believed that. You should have been more sensitive to your wife, too. I am a wise woman, but I have always wanted to tell you that." She turned in her floral dress and pushed the weird-legged thing across a roomful of people, and then she turned around and humped it back. "I can't stand myself behaving that way, Chester. Please accept my apologies. It has been a long life, and I am concerned about what you are doing there on that farm. This church is not one for gossip, but we have all been concerned." Bags under her eyes were triple folded. She looked like a blood hound.

"I'm doing fine," Chet said.

"That's not what I hear. I hear that you never clean

the place up and that you wander around your cow pastures in some kind of, I don't know, some kind of stupor or something. You have to get over it, Chester. Lois is in heaven now, and you have to get over it. Some of us in this church would like to help. It's very good you came to church and came to Simon's party."

"What else have you heard?" Chet asked.

"Oh, we've heard that you never go to the bank and you need a new roof. And your place cleaned up. And I'll bet if I talked to a few people, they'd be more than happy to help." She banged her walker around to rotate herself. "Where's Walt? Walter!"

Higgins tottered over with a moving bulge in his jacket pocket. "Chet!" he said. "You're looking dapper tonight!" One of his repulsive ferrets nosed its head out of Walter's pocket, twitched its whiskers, and went back inside.

"Walt," Harriet Bertram said, "I was thinking we might get some folks together to help Chet out at home. We all help each other, but Chet hasn't had much help since Lois passed on."

Walt stuck a hand in his pocket, cried out, and wiped a bloody finger on his lapel. "Sure, yes, we should help Chet out."

"I could straighten and organize his kitchen and his little domestic gadgets," Harriet said. "Maybe some of you boys could help with the roof." She turned to Chet. "You may not remember this, but Walt is renowned for his carpentry. He is a veritable artisan with hammer and saw."

"Can't do much of it anymore," Walter said, "but I could get the newest member of the congregation to help—hey, his name's Chester too!"

"Yeah," Harriet said. "It's kind of like we got another Chester when the old one didn't come around anymore."

Chet looked across the room. The Other Chet raised a glass at him and laughed.

"I was wondering," Chet said to both of them, and they gazed at him expectantly. "I was thinking about how this other Chester not only has my name, but looks an awful lot like me, to an eerie extent." Harriet and Walt looked around. "He's over by the rocking chair," Chet tried to whisper, but at that moment the blue dress woman began banging out "God Bless America" on the piano, so that Harriet and Walt squinted helplessly at odd corners of the room.

"In any case, Chet," Walter said—the ferret leaped from his pocket to the floor and ran away—"Chet, I will call you. Make no mistake. I think this idea of Harriet's is a splendid one. I will call you. We can get a whole crew to come and help you out." After that, Walt brought several glasses of wine to Chet, and the Other Chester offered to drive him home.

They sat on the sofa in the farm house, and the Other Chester said, "You know, I think you and I could have a lot in common." Geordie was flopped in a corner with a concerned expression on his face as he looked at the Other Chet. They'd brought a couple of full bottles of wine back from Simon Bone's.

"Like what?"

"Like I always wanted to live on a farm."

"I always wanted to get off the farm, but I never did," Chet said. "Never got off the farm, but that's good. Lois liked it here."

"So that's something we kind of have in common. Being in some place we didn't want to be, or so we thought." This young upstart Other looked distracted, but he was still coherent. "And then we wind up at the same church."

"It's not the same church," Chet replied quickly. "It's not the same at all."

"Well it is, and I guess it isn't, in a way. Churches must

change over time."

Chet said, "Not that much. They shouldn't change that much. Nope."

"Have some wine."

"Thank you."

"Saturday they'll come to fix this place up. The people from the congregation—Harriet, Walter, and some friends. And of course I'll be here." The Other Chet's face looked happy in the dim light of the 40-watt bulb in the living room lamp. He looked genuinely happy.

"You could be my son," Chet said, feeling comfortable. "You actually could be. You look like me. You have my name."

"Yes, it is a coincidence," the Other said.

"But I already have a son. I think he wants to put me away in an old man's home or something. I really suspect it."

"My God!" The Other said. "My God, that's horrible. You are getting up there in years, Chet, but you aren't out of it yet. By God, no. Don't let him do it, do you hear me? You just call someone, me, Walter, Simon Bone, anyone, but don't you let him do it!"

"I won't," Chet said. "Damned if I'll let him do it. If he tries again, I'll get you or Harriet or Walt or someone on the horn. I'll tell you what's going on."

"Good. Just remember it."

"I will." Chet slammed back the rest of his glass of wine.

The Other Chet started to pick his face and to doze on the sofa. Chet got up on his wobbly legs and searched the linen closet for a blanket. He straightened out the kid's knees and legs so that he was at rest and then tossed the scratchy blanket over him.

Is this what I used to look like in sleep? Chet wondered. The Other Chet's eyelashes looked like fans on his cheeks.

The Other Chet was gone the next morning; the blanket slouched on the dog-haired floor by the sofa. Chet remembered it was Friday, and people were supposed to come to see him on Saturday, so he spent Friday collecting stones, oak branches, wildflower stalks, and other things to build a monument to his wife among the grasses and thick cow pies. He had gotten a few large timbers into the ground, and he embellished these with pliant plants and sticks. He re-crossed the road to his porch after that and regarded his work from his rocking chair. The rest of the day he spent sleeping in the silt filled air of his and Lois' room, on the clean part of the bedspread warmed by the sun.

Saturday afternoon brought a whole host of people in the sandeye-rubbing morning in Illinois: There was of course the Other Chester, with Walter Higgins minus his ferrets; and Harriet Bertram with a few matronly kitchen tinkers; and there was of course Simon Bone himself, flanked with a few hardware-pierced fledglings from the Youth Group; and there were also strays who brought (as upon Lois's death) green bean casseroles, vegetable molded jellos, and suspect pies. Sonny arrived also, coincidentally, for as Simon Bone questioned, who knows about these things?

Harriet and her flock disassembled kitchen drawers and arranged buckets and rusty garden tools in the shed outside. Chet worried a little that they'd find his money hiding place in the kitchen pantry but they seemed oblivious to it. Harriet dusted boxes and jars in the pantry with a pair of Chet's underwear. She put safety pins to various uses. Sonny creaked around on the roof with Simon Bone for awhile and made major construction noises, banging on rafters with hammers and drilling in mysterious places. Chet felt the edges of his character erode. The whole farm was as out of control as a crashing aircraft; stick bodies were everywhere, and he went outside. The pink-brown lizards, their delicate toe-holds gripping the edges of the porch, watched him with intensity, and the sigh of the oboe came from below. Lois' shape appeared near where he'd started building his altar. She wore her white hair down as if she were going to bed, and the hem of her nightgown brushed the grasses and sticks of the field. Late sunlight showed the silhouette of her body through lace. It was intact. He cried out to her, and she dissipated like a vapor, the way a funnel cloud joins clear air.

And this is when they came for him: Sonny, Harriet, the Other Chet, Walter, kids, the whole lot, like wasps from the house. A kid from the youth group started the car. Sonny had Chet's old duffel bag already packed.

SURVIVAL

A ll you do," said Graham, rubbing the lenses of his glasses on his T-shirt, "is turn it on, click on the software, click CONNECT, and away you go." He pulled a low stool up to the kitchen desk where the computer was. "You'll hear a dialing noise, then a beeping noise, then a fax kind of noise, then you'll connect." He stroked a thin beard.

Thursa looked almost young. "And then the ethereal characters?" she said hopefully, wringing a kitchen towel.

"Yeah. If we can't get you out of the house, then I guess you'll have to talk to them. Maybe then you won't be so lonely."

"I get out of the house," said Thursa, gazing at the computer screen. "I take Tiger out. I do the marketing. I pick the cherries."

"And fall on your ass off a ladder," said her son.

"Graham! That only happened once. The cherries are vital." Her hand alighted on the mouse.

"To what? Vital to what?"

The mouse pointer approached the cyberspace software icon on the screen. "Yeah," she said, sarcastically. "Ask me that when they're ripe. Little Red Hen."

"What?"

"I'm the Little Red Hen," she said. Her index finger was poised to drop on the mouse button. The pointer was over the icon.

"Mother, you are seventy-three and should not be on a ladder," he said. Then decided to cheer her. "So are you ready? For cyberspace?"

Thursa's knotted fingers jerked away from the mouse. "No," she said. "Not now. Tonight. When it's dark." She nodded sharply. "That's when I shall experience the ethereal characters."

◆

Thursa wore Dockers and lived in mountainous country with a retriever who refused to swim. She housed a pacemaker and smoked cigarettes, and after the gardening and the news there was nothing to do. Wipe the counter. Turn up the heat. Keeping track of weather and temperature were vital, because she made long distance phone calls and told people about them. A few years back she had volunteered for Audubon, but now she was getting tired.

When the sun went down that Tuesday night, and the night insects hummed through her window screens, she plugged cream-colored candles into Waterford candlesticks and lit them. She walked softly over to the computer in her Peds.

Tiger followed her.

She turned on the computer and clicked on the icon.

She clicked CONNECT.

There were no characters at first. She tentatively investigated and followed directions, and then she gasped.

"Tiger!" she said. "There's an art forum! Tiger, you don't know it, but I used to paint!"

GO ART, she typed. She hit RETURN. "And who," she said to Tiger, "could be more ethereal than artists?"

An artistic logo appeared on her screen, and there was a message asking her if she would like to join the forum. She typed in her name.

On the menu above, it said "messages," and below that, "browse." She slid the mouse pointer to "browse." The pointer became an hourglass. When she moved it in circles and figure eights, a nervous habit of hers, many hourglasses appeared in succession following the first one, and then vanished! She loved that aspect of her computer.

"If the clan in Wisconsin could see me now," she said to Tiger. "If any of them was alive. But maybe they can see me. See us," she said.

A list of artistic topics popped up on the screen. Thursa blinked her green eyes in amazement. She left the mouse for a minute and tottered over to fix herself a bourbon. Then she was back.

"Oh, here's a Seranno topic. It'll be about the 'Piss Christ' thing," she said. She knew this from reading a news magazine. "It offended the Catholics, you know," she asserted, looking at Tiger. "Tax money for a crucifix in urine. They did not like it." She clicked on the topic.

Thursa's first glimpse of a character appeared in the form of a note about Seranno's use of light both in the glass of urine and on the crucifix. She considered this, remembering what she could of the piece. She sipped her bourbon and stared at the screen. She lit a cigarette. Numbers in the upper left corner of the screen ticked the time away.

"I thought it was good," she said to Tiger. "Subject aside, the use of light was very good. There was almost a glowing quality to the glass, in places."

There was a button marked REPLY at the lower edge of the message. She clicked on it and typed in what she thought as she had described it to Tiger. Then she clicked one that said SEND.

There was also a button that said MORE, and she tried that one. Another message appeared.

WHO THE HELL CARES ABOUT WHAT THE SON OF A BITCH DID HE DEGRADED JESUS

CHRIST AND CHRISTIANITY AND THE JUDEO-
CHRISTIAN TRADITION OF THIS COUNTRY AND
WE HAVE TO STOP THIS KIND OF SHIT FROM
EVER HAPPENING AGAIN. VOTE REPUBLICAN!!

"Well!" said Thursa. "That's not necessary." She looked at her dog. "Must be a Catholic character," she said.

Just then a small box popped up on her computer screen, and some text within it.

HELLO THURSA!

It said.

AND HOW ARE YOU ON THIS ROMANTIC AND STAR-
RY EVENING?

She gasped. Her right hand left the mouse and went to her heart, over where the pacemaker was. "Dear God!" she said to Tiger. She turned the computer off without bothering to exit the program. She regarded the blank screen for a second, half expecting it to light on its own.

"They really are alive!" she said.

The candlelight threw her wavering shadow onto a wall. She looked out the window to the night sky. There were no stars.

✦

The next morning, Tiger's scratching and flatulence on Thursa's bed brought her awake as the sun was shining through some natural-weave curtains that covered her bedroom window. He rolled, grunted, and bombed. She lit a cigarette, then put on slippers and her bathrobe and went to the kitchen to put coffee on.

As she shuffled past the computer she tried not to look at it, but curiosity overcame her. The screen was blank.

She fixed herself some toast and orange juice, and pretty soon Tiger stiffly entered the kitchen and stretched. She let him outside.

It was early enough that the birds were still calling to each other and winging in arcs. Stellar's jays were hanging upside down from the rope on her feeder trying to get sunflower seeds. They were too heavy to perch on the feeder. They clowned and squawked away chickadees and finches.

"Ornithology!" she said to Tiger, even though he was outside. "Maybe an ornithology forum! I could contribute to that, and maybe be a member of the art forum as well—Tiger?"

He was standing outside at the sliding screen door.

"Tiger, get in here," she said, letting him back in.

✦

"No, Mother," said Graham over the phone. "I don't think it was a pervert. I think it was another artist, like yourself, who wanted to talk to you." She heard sleepy sighs from him and questionable noises from his wife. She hated to wake them.

"Then how do you explain the starry, romantic evening part?" Thursa said. She had the TV news on and watched it out of a corner of her eye. She was waiting for the weather. She had hesitantly unplugged the modem to plug in the phone and was drinking her third cup of coffee.

"I don't know," he said. She heard noises of sheets, of soft movement. "Ethereal characters talk like that. Was it a woman or a man?"

"I don't know. Can you tell?"

"Yeah. There should be a name at the top of the box. If you want to answer, type something and press return. Do artists talk that way?"

Thursa stirred her coffee and considered this. "Yes.

Sometimes they do."

"O-kay. So you're all set. So you can let me get on with my day," he said.

Thursa thought she knew what he wanted to get on with.

✦

Thursa was preoccupied, so much so that she forgot which aisle in the grocery store the Milk Bones were in. A jar of marmalade slipped from her arthritic fingers and splashed orange on the floor, and she laughed.

When she took Tiger on his daily walk, she went a different way and ended up in a stranger's back yard. A possum scuffled on top of a length of fence there. Tiger strained at his leash and barked, making small leaps in the little animal's direction. It dropped from the fence and wiggled under a woodpile.

Thursa was elated. "Oh Tiger, isn't that creature an anachronism?" And then she said, "What am I going to do with you?" in mock anger to Tiger, and she jerked the leash on his choke collar. Her eyes sparkled.

Thursa trimmed her azalea and was proud of her work.

She eagerly got her mail and paused over a solicitation from the Sierra Club, and then it was time to eat dinner. She microwaved a frozen macaroni and cheese dinner. She giggled and ate it out of the box.

It was getting dark. She could stand it no longer. This time she fixed herself a whiskey before she turned on her computer and lit the candles. She exchanged the stool for a hard-backed chair with a pad and made herself comfortable.

She clicked the icon.

She clicked CONNECT.

GO ART . . .

    TO: ALL

WILL THE KIND ARTIST WHO CONTACTED ME
AND MENTIONED THE STARRY ROMANTIC EVE-
NING PLEASE CONTACT ME AGAIN? I DID NOT
MEAN TO BE RUDE. I AM AN ELDERLY WOMAN
AND NEW AT THIS.
                    —THURSA BURNS

She browsed messages and responded to some with some general questions:

WHAT IS WYETH'S "THE VIRGIN" LIKE?
and
WHERE IS MONET'S "SUNFLOWERS" NOW?

She fixed herself another whiskey. She thought about how oil painting, at close view, seemed a meaningless jumble of daubs of color, but at a farther range sprang to life in a coalescence of light.

The artists were ethereal. They spoke of shapes, textures, colors, perspectives, and emotions. They got angry sometimes and shouted in capital letters.

"Our subjects range far and wide," she said, winking at Tiger. She was a little drunk. "It's time to dust off my art books and pick up a brush once more."

✦

"The ornithology people," Thursa said one evening, "are somewhat like the artists in ethereal qualities, but more scientific in their way of looking at things. And I for one am glad to be a part of it. Take, for example, the method of examining the eye rings on the birds. The eye rings can be vital in identification, but the artist would note them for a different reason."

Thursa's white hair stuck out in all directions. She had

not brushed it in days. Cherries had fallen from the tree and were getting eaten by the birds. She lit another cigarette.

And then after her exit from the ornithology forum, as she entered the art forum, a message appeared at the bottom of the screen. It said:

YOU HAVE WAITING MESSAGES.

✦

MY NAME IS HACK (HAROLD). I AM THE ART-
IST WHO SENT YOU THE MESSAGE ABOUT THE
STARS. I TOO AM AN ELDERLY ARTISTS! WHAT
MEDIUM OR MEDIA DO YOU USE? HOW LONG
HAVE YOU BEEN AN ARTIST? HAVE YOU BEEN
TO ANY GOOD SHOWS LATELY? SOMETIMES
I SCULPT OTHERS I PAINT (OIL). WHERE DO
YOU LIVE? I HAVE AN ARTICLE ABOUT THE
METROPOLITAN MUSEUM OF ART WHICH MAY
INTEREST YOU(?) IF SO, PLEASE RESPOND WITH
YOUR ADDRESS. I AM IN WASHINGTON.

—HACK

P.S. I ALSO HAVE AN AFFINITY FOR GOLF.

Thursa froze, stiff as a cricket. Who was this man, really? Should she respond? Maybe he was an artist/politician, in which case she did not want to reply. On the other hand, an article of that kind would bring her closer in touch with the art forum people.

She clicked the REPLY button, and typed in her address.

✦

"I was just wondering," said Graham over the phone,

"why you didn't have us over for Sunday dinner and cherry pie."

Thursa put some finishing touches of fuzz on a peach she was painting. A glob of paint hit the floor. "Oh damn," she said.

"Mother?"

"Oh, yes Graham." She put her brush down and hobbled over to seize a dish cloth and bent over laboriously to wipe up the paint. "Yes, I've just been so busy. And remember what I told you about the Little Red Hen. 'And who will help me grind the flour?' said the Little Red Hen."

"What are you doing?"

"I'm painting again, Graham. And it's very tiring. I didn't have the time to do the cherries or the dinner or anything else. I've just been busy."

"Just wanted to make sure you're all right."

Thursa giggled. "I'm fine!" she said. She flipped the computer on with her free hand.

✦

She was in the ornithology forum.

SHEILA:
IN AUTUMN, I HAVE TOWHEES GRUBBING
THROUGH LEAVES, GOING BACKWARDS

she wrote.

Almost immediately, she got a message back.

THURSA, YOU DON'T EVEN KNOW WHAT A
TOWHEE LOOKS LIKE. THE TOWHEES ARE
MY TERRITORY HERE IN THE FORUM. I'VE
PRACTICALLY RAISED TOWHEES AND HAVE

NURSED FLEDGLINGS INTO ADULTHOOD.
THEY NEVER GO BACKWARDS. PLEASE DO NOT
BOTHER FORUM MEMBERS ANY LONGER WITH
YOUR MISINFORMATION.
—SHEILA

Thursa chewed a stubby thumbnail in the wavering light of the candles as the message sank in. Her eyes overflowed with tears. Was this woman implying that she was senile? That she didn't know what she was talking about? She knew what she saw, and she had seen the towhees lurching jerkily backwards through the leaves.

And then a hideous thought occurred to her. Other people in the forum, browsing the messages, would read the message Sheila had sent!

A speedy reply was vital.

DEAR SHEILA,

she wrote,

I SUPPOSE YOU WILL ALSO TELL ME THAT I
HAVE NOT SEEN A WHITE-BREASTED NUT-
HATCH GOING HEADFIRST DOWN A TREE, AND
THAT YOU ARE AN EXPERT ON THOSE, TOO.
—THURSA BURNS

Thursa exited the forum, but stayed online. To disconnect completely would be to admit defeat. She sat in front of her computer and felt exhausted suddenly, except for an electric surge of nervous energy, like a hot wire, which lay beneath her surface. Sleep would be impossible. The windows she had opened for fresh air yielded a clawing humidity and it was hard to breathe. Her muscles and skin felt tender.

When she re-entered the forum fifteen minutes later, a message was waiting.

It was from Sheila.

THURSA:

YOU PROBABLY SEE ALL KINDS OF THINGS. YOU ARE PROBABLY A BORED AND SHALL WE SAY IMAGINATIVE OLD WOMAN WHO HAS NOTHING BETTER TO DO THAN TO REFUTE THE FACTS OF THE SPECIES DISCUSSED IN THIS FORUM. BUT IT IS MISLEADING TO MANY WHO ARE NEW HERE. ONCE AGAIN I WILL ASK YOU TO REFRAIN FROM YOUR MISGUIDED CONTRIBUTIONS. THIS IS THE LAST TIME.

—SHEILA

P.S. I BROWSE THE ART FORUM. I KNOW WHERE YOU LIVE.

Thursa felt at once terribly weak. Why would Sheila care where she lived? Was it because of bird habitat, or because of something else?

She thought she heard the sound of snapping sticks outside.

Her electrical energy left her with a rush. Thursa's head hit the keyboard like a heavy melon.

Then there was nothing.

✦

When Graham woke her she was still on-line, and Sheila's message was still on the screen. Graham pushed his glasses up on his nose and squinted at it as Thursa adjusted her mental bearings. He had tried to call her and her line had been busy for hours.

"I don't think the ethereal characters were such a good idea," he said.

Thursa was still groggy. "I have to reply to the message in the ornithology forum."

"No you don't," he said. He hesitated and said, "This whole thing has flipped you out. Getting out of the house more would be a better idea." He gently touched the area of her forehead that had hit the keyboard, and went to the refrigerator for some ice. "I'm going to delete the software," he said.

She took the ice from him. It was wrapped in a towel. "You don't have to do that," she said. "I don't think I'll be going back online. I have cherries to pick—oh God, the cherries! And I have Sunday dinners to cook, and things to do. I really have no business painting, either. But I'd like to save and savor the messages I have in my files. The good ones."

Graham shrugged. "I'm going to have to take you to the hospital now Mother." He sighed. "I think this might have something to do with your heart."

✦

The cherries had rotted to slush in the yard under and around the tree. On a sunny day Thursa put on her straw hat and raked the mess into a few piles. She clucked like a chicken. "Little Red Hen," she said.

Graham pulled the modem from her computer, but left the software intact, as promised. He helped her pack her paint and her brushes and put them in boxes in the basement.

When he left she scraped candle wax from the kitchen counter and checked the weather.

There was nothing wrong with her heart that wasn't wrong already, the doctor said, but there would be plenty very soon if she didn't quit smoking. How could a woman so in tune with the natural world, the doctor had asked rhetorically, act so irresponsibly with her own body?

This had reminded Thursa of the tone of Sheila's last message in the ornithology forum and she had hung her head. At least the doctor's message had been private.

✦

Two weeks later, Thursa tossed a bag of dog food into her shopping basket. It crunched when it landed. She grimaced at an arthritic stab from her right shoulder.

A young woman stood about four feet down the aisle, studying the label on a can of cat food.

"Shit I hate this place," she said to the woman.

She took Tiger on his walk, and nothing eventful happened. It rained. "We won't even bother checking for the anachronism," she said to Tiger. "He won't be there."

When the mail came she didn't even open the brown paper cover on the National Geographic.

With large hedge clippers, she overpruned the lilac down to stubby twigs.

She sat at the kitchen table and added to her lists of things to do, erasing some and rewriting. She clenched her teeth as she sharpened the pencil several times with a little red sharpener, and she rubbed her eyes.

After she had fixed herself a tossed salad for dinner, she wearily set herself a place at the table. She ate some dry bread with it. There was a spatter of red paint on the table, and she scratched it off with her fingernail.

✦

The next day, to her own surprise, she almost kicked Tiger after their walk. He had been enough before. Now she almost resented him, this dog of a lonely old woman.

But she forgot all about him when she drew single envelope from the mailbox. It was a letter for her from H. Showers in the state of Washington. It was stained with coffee.

When she opened it she found the article about the Metropolitan Museum of Art in New York, and with it was a scrawled note that said: "Where are you Thursa? What happened to you? All of us in the forum miss your messages and your curiosity. Please join us back on-line soon." It was signed "Hack."

Thursa sat on her floral sofa with the article and note in her lap and stared into space. "I don't know!" she whispered to Tiger, who lay at her feet. "I just don't know!"

✦

Thursa was on a ladder, digging through scarves and hats on the top shelf of the hall closet. "The key," she said to Tiger, "to this whole affair, is to find the modem. Graham hid it, I know he did, but if we can find it I'm sure we can hook it up." Alarm crossed her face. "What if he took it with him?"

Just as she said this, her fingers clamped around a hard, rectangular box, and she knew she had it. All of the necessary connections were there. The timing was perfect. It was almost dark.

✦

Thursa impatiently threw the hourglass around the screen. She swilled her small glass of bourbon in the candlelight. When the software icon appeared, she clicked on it.

She clicked CONNECT.

GO ART . . .

There were twenty-five messages waiting for her in the art forum, and twenty in ornithology. They had missed her. Before she could collect her messages though, a small blue box appeared on the screen. It said:

HELLO THURSA! AND HOW ARE YOU ON THIS ROMANTIC AND STORMY NIGHT?

Thursa laughed in delight and looked out her window at a sky that glittered with stars. She waxed ethereal, and hastened to reply.

COYOTE

Old age was to Oscar an indication of just how fragile a human being was, especially when he caught sight of himself naked in the mirror at the end of the hall. His chest, which was broad and reasonably deep when he was young, was wisped with gray hair and hollow as a beehive. There was not much in the way of muscle left in his legs, which would have looked like sticks had they not been curved and bowed. Most of his teeth had left him in the past five years. He'd recently become petrified of falling, because old people usually fell and shattered something brittle before they died, and so he began to walk peculiarly and deliberately on the balls of his feet, tiptoeing around the old men's home both at night and in the yellow light of day. The cushioned walk felt somehow safer, steadier, but Thomas, the very dark black man who shared Oscar's room, laughed at him openly with every step he took. Yet it wasn't until Oscar had fully resigned himself to the fact that he was finally an old man that he was jolted into the complexity of youth again; it wasn't until Oscar hit 70 that he finally fell in love.

The old men's home wasn't so much cleaned as it was disinfected. Dirt collected on the baseboards, under the television set and on the table downstairs in the lounge, around dusty window panes and the peeling panels of doors. Grease spots from the oils of old man heads blossomed and bled on upholstered wing chairs. The cleaning lady was at least half blind, but her nose worked, so that a bathroom sprinkled with mold might throw the pungent scent of Pine Sol into the hall, or even down the filthy or-ange-runnered stairs.

Yet if the place hadn't been filthy, Oscar might not have noticed Jane (although not to have noticed her would have been difficult), because she commented on it the minute she stepped through the front door with her daughter. She said, "Wow, this place is a mess!" She didn't say it as if she would explode, and she didn't whine. She said it with apparent disbelief, and her eyes waxed round. She absently pushed strands of white hair away from her face to where it had been loosely pinned to her head. She had a deeply tanned face that was probably only a few years younger than Oscar's but which seemed timeless. She wore a necklace of beads and feathers over a long, flowered cotton dress.

Oscar had been ball-footing it carefully down the hall like a dancer. He lowered his weight back down to his heels of his boots and touched the wall for balance, be-cause his stick legs went to feeling like Jello the minute he saw her, and he caught his breath and felt his heart, be-cause he had been married four times, but none of those times had Oscar had such an instant, familiar reaction as this. He was scared as hell.

✦

Her daughter stood by the front door in a leather vest and torn sandals. Her face was round like her mother's but her eyes were blue. "It looks like there's all guys in here," she said.

Her mother looked around, from left to right. "Why you're right!" she said. "Where are the other women here?"

Leroy staggered up with authority, his chest like a bar-rel. He was comparatively fit because he was fifty-three, and he lorded this over all of the men in his old man's home just by walking around with his chest puffed out. "No women here," he said.

The daughter frowned and thought a minute. "Is that legal?" she said.

"Daisy, it probably is," the beautiful woman said. "They probably found some loophole, and now they're living like a bunch of school boys in a frat house here with all this dirt!" And she doubled over and laughed, loud, nodding and smiling at Leroy, a couple of other oldsters playing spades at the table in the lounge, and even down the hall to where Oscar leaned up against a door frame. His face grew hot when she noticed him. She looked at him only briefly, however, and seemed unaware of the men playing spades, too, who were gaping at her sporadically from their hairy hands of cards and glancing sideways at her as they tossed cards onto the table in play. Oscar felt like an animal when he realized they were looking at her too. He felt like a goddam animal.

"It's legal," Leroy said. He pulled a toothpick from his T-shirt pocket and wedged it back behind a molar. "It's my old man's home, and I can do whatever I want with it, and I can let anybody in I want." Oscar noticed he stood with his tattooed arm positioned away from the beautiful woman.

"Well my name's Jane, and this is my daughter Daisy, and I need a place to stay. I can't stay with Daisy anymore, and my husband's in a full-care nursing facility, and it is costing me an arm and a leg, so I need some kind of cheap housing accommodation. Do you understand?" Her tan accentuated her powder-green eyes, and they brightened when she wanted him to understand. Oscar admired this at the same time his heart cracked in two at the mention of her husband.

"By the way," Jane said. "When I said it was costing an

arm and a leg, was I making an especially sick pun?"

Leroy looked at her and it was clear he did not understand.

She squinted and looked at the floor. "I probably did."

"You did," Daisy said.

◆

So Leroy made her sit on the ripped pink couch with her purse in her lap next to Daisy for at least half an hour while he thought this whole thing over, but it didn't seem to bother her much. She and Daisy both pulled books from their respective baggage of purses and began to read, and Jane asked Leroy if he had any coffee, but then clapped a hand over her mouth as if the very request might hurt her chances of being admitted to the old men's home. It struck Oscar in the meantime that he might resemble a pervert, lurking in the hall like that, and so he went to take a pee in the aqua bathroom, went to his room to don his turquoise and silver bolo tie, and then tiptoed back to take a chair in the lounge and pretend to read *The Denver Post*. The paper shook like aspen leaves in a blizzard so he steadied it by resting his forearms on his knees. Jane would think he had Parkinson's disease, old man that he was. And that's one thing he didn't have, at least not yet.

Then Oscar began to realize the possibilities which lay before him. This beautiful girl was waiting to find out if she could live where he lived! The whole thing was too incredible for him to comprehend. She sat on the ripped pink couch in her dress with the purple flowers, reading her book (and Oscar could tell she liked to read), but it was Leroy who held the keys to the fate that lay ahead. Leroy was the one. Oscar looked up from his paper at the two women, and Jane looked up right as he did, right at him. Her eyes were electric, and she was bashful and happy to look at him, and looked down at her book again. Oscar tried to read the title of the book from where he sat but couldn't because her fingers covered the print. He remembered Leroy again, pushed himself up out of his chair, and went to the kitchen after Leroy and pushed open the swinging door.

He put his hands on the thin hips of his Levis. "She can have my room," he said. "And we got two empty rooms if mine's not good enough. Only you don't let anybody use those rooms."

Leroy was eating puffed rice cereal from a plastic bag. A few greasy locks of gray-black hair fell over his forehead, and he looked like a nasty adolescent. "We can't have a woman in here," he said.

"Why not?"

"Because there ain't never been any woman in here," said Leroy. "It'd drive the old men crazy and they'd start doing stupid things."

"They'd be cleaner. And she could tell the blind woman when she missed a spot," Oscar said, logically. "She could help out. I know she would."

"You know her?"

"Kind of."

"She one of them wives you had?"

"Fuck you," said Oscar. He went over to the Mr. Coffee and poured a hot cup in the only clean mug he could find. There was no cream or sugar and he hoped she took it black.

"I'll think about it a few more minutes," Leroy said, through a mash of puffed rice. He laughed.

Oscar took the coffee to Jane and she nodded in appreciation, but she blushed and looked back at her book. There was no place to set the coffee cup so he put it on the floor at her feet. Oscar resumed his position in the chair and tried not to grunt like an old man as he sat down, and when he started looking at the paper again it was impossible to read. But when he looked up once she was staring at him.

Then Leroy dramatically bashed open the swinging door to the kitchen and banged his ostrich boots on the hardwood floor as he approached her, his chest puffed out. He stood directly in front of her, his thumbs through the belt loops of his jeans like a stud, and said "I have decided." The men playing spades put down their cards. Oscar pushed the newspaper up in front of his face and listened carefully. "I have decided you can stay if you pay a little more than the men, because women are messier and more trouble, and if you help the cleaning lady by showing her where to clean."

"How much more?" Jane said.

"A hundred or so," said Leroy. "Your room will have to be the one at the end of the hall, and you have to take your bath at night so you don't run into the geezers on their way in and out of there."

"I wouldn't want to do anything like that," Jane said, and from behind his paper Oscar understood; she was making fun of Leroy, but Leroy didn't catch on.

"I only say that for your benefit, because it ain't pleasant," Leroy said.

"Right," she said. The room smelled just a little bit like flowers, and a few minutes later Oscar heard her say she'd move in the next day.

✦

Thomas lay on his back on his patchwork bedspread, taking a nap with his boots still on and a Stetson covering his face. He didn't stir until Oscar paced up and down the room, and then sat on his own bed only to get up and pace some more. He pushed the hat aside enough so that one of his big brown eyes showed, and said "What's the matter with you, Oscar?"

"I know this sounds ridiculous, but I think I am in love," Oscar said seriously.

"Hah! Well it won't be the first time, from what you said." Thomas crossed his feet at the ankles and pushed the hat over his face again.

"No, I mean actually in love," said Oscar. "Not in lust or lusting after wanting to be a husband, but in love," he said. "She's moving in tomorrow, and I don't know what to do."

Thomas slowly took the hat from his face and sat up, his boots hitting the floor. He looked at Oscar with concern. "You all right, man?"

"Oh fuck I don't know," Oscar said. "I am so weak, you know? I'm so old and so weak."

"You'll be all right."

Oscar looked at Thomas in exasperation. "No. I won't be all right. This woman is moving in, and I think I'm in love with her, love at first sight, but it's all wrong, cause she's married." He sat on the edge of his bed and pulled out a pint of Jack from underneath it, unscrewed the cap, and took a swig. He gazed at the floor and pictured Jane's old man in a crank-up bed, with hoses and tubes and wires running to and from his body, down his nose, down his throat, into his veins, over his heart, from his dick into a rubber bag; a virtual corpse who may or may not recognize his own wife and want her to sit softly beside him. He heard the beeping and droning of electronics, signaling the various pulsating whispers of what passed for Jane's husband's life. Perhaps even a large hose entered his throat and inflated his lungs with the rushing sound of air.

"Oh," said Thomas. And he put his chin in his hands and looked at the floor too. "Well then why's she moving in here?"

"Her old man's in a nursing home."

"Oh!" Thomas said again. "I mean you wouldn't—"

"No, I wouldn't," said Oscar. He passed the bottle to Thomas' outstretched hand.

✦

The day Jane moved in, the ashtrays on the card table were overflowing with butts, and Oscar emptied these hurriedly even while a card game was going on, to the astonishment of the players, who held on to their coffee cups. Oscar was sure that from this day on things would never be the same in the old men's home, but he didn't know exactly how things would change or what other changes those changes might bring. When he thought about how old he was, change scared him.

The first change was of course the presence of Jane herself, which was like a summer day in the middle of February. She arrived wearing a straw hat decorated with dried fruits (which would have looked ridiculous on any other woman, but which looked astonishingly beautiful on Jane), and she carried a couple of small flowering plants, her bulbous-ended fingers wrapped around their painted flower pots. Periodically she turned to stare at Oscar. There was a huge amount of activity with rags, cleaners, and mops in Jane's new room before her belongings crossed its threshold.

When he gathered up enough courage to look in she was standing on a chair, hanging something from her curtain rod in front of the window. It looked like a crude rendition of the woven part of a tennis racquet or a snow shoe, decorated with feathers and colored beads, and it dangled in the light that came in from the window. She secured a knot deftly with her tan hands and said without turning around, "It's a dream catcher. It catches the animals in your dreams."

"Yeah?" said Oscar.

"Animal dreams were very important to the Indians," she said. "Every dream animal is significant. I can show you a list of what each animal means." She stepped daintily down from the chair and turned around to face him. "Would you like one?"

"I don't know!" Oscar said. "Why? Do you have an extra one?"

She nodded and smiled excitedly, and went to the closet. She reached inside and then brought one over to him. "This one's bigger!" she said. "The webbing in the middle catches the bad dreams during the night, and they evaporate with the sun in the morning. The good dreams pass right on through." The dream catcher was huge, bigger than a garbage can lid. Large eagle feathers and blue and gold beads hung from it on thick strands of leather. "Hang it from your curtain rod, if it's close to your bed," she whispered.

Oscar was not eager to stand on a chair in his room and risk the shattering of his brittle bones. "I don't have a chair in my room," he said.

"Then we can use this one," she said, pointing to the folding chair she'd been using. "And don't worry, you won't fall. No one has fallen hanging up a dream catcher." She dragged the chair to his room, climbed on top of it, and motioned for him to give her the dream catcher. After she'd hung it, she stepped down from the chair and back to admire it, and she pinned some loose strands of white hair back into place on her head.

She smiled wide at Oscar, reached her hand out toward his face, and then suddenly looked at the floor and started walking back to her room. Oscar wondered with a pang if she had put a dream catcher over her husband's bed in the nursing home. Just then Leroy appeared and stared at Oscar's dream catcher. "I told you a woman would start some shit," he said. "And I can see it's already begun."

✦

That night, Oscar retired early and had the coyote dream. Coyotes surrounded him under a glowing jar-lid of a moon on the ranch he used to own, and he was trying to shoot them with a .22 lever-action rifle to protect his livestock. But each time he aimed to fire at one, it howled behind him and another one appeared with yellow laughing eyes. He was so old in the dream that it took all of his strength just to shoulder the rifle, and he heard his leg bones cracking as coyote after coyote dropped into his dream. There were hundreds of them.

"Oscar?" Thomas said.

Oscar woke and looked at the dream catcher, hoping the dream was lodged there securely. Thomas stared at the dream catcher too and then looked down at Oscar again.

"Last night Jane told me to give you this card. It has something to do with animals, lists of animals. What's that over your bed, man?"

Oscar grabbed the card, rubbed his eyes, and scanned it for COYOTE. "Here it is, Thomas," he said. "Listen to this. 'Humor, trickster, reversal of fortune, folly.' Thomas, I shouldn't be in love with this woman. What the fuck am I doing?"

"I don't know!" Thomas said, earnestly. "But this afternoon I thought you, me, and Jane would go on down to the Berkeley for a beer. She's a real nice lady, Oscar. I talked to her a little bit last night."

"I can't go near her," Oscar said. "But I can't stay away from her either!" He rose unsteadily in his boxer shorts and walked on the balls of his feet over to the closet for his bathrobe. "There must be some way I can condition myself not to care," he said. He rubbed his eyes and padded to the bathroom for a shower.

✦

When Thomas, Jane, and Oscar went out for beer, Jane wore green glass beads, which she fingered incessantly as she listened to the details of Oscar's dream. It was difficult for him to speak to her; as usual, her very presence brought knots to his throat, and telling her about his dream was personal and made things even worse. It was hard for him to express the dream-fear the coyotes conjured up on that night, but then dream-fear was always, for Oscar, on a par with his fear of old age and of weakness.

Jane was shocked that the coyote figured in his dreams. She put one of her soft, tan hands on one of Oscar's, and he thought he would faint. When she did this, Thomas eyed both her and Oscar gravely, adding to the sense of mystery and even possible doom which was beginning to pervade their little table. Thomas readjusted his hat.

"The coyote," said Jane, "is the divine trickster! He often brings a frightened feeling to a dream. He is ..." she paused. "He is the ultimate cosmic joke."

"Does that mean I'm a joke?" said Oscar. He suddenly wondered if he had effectively insulted himself by mentioning the coyote in the first place.

"Oh, no," she said, patting his hand again. "It simply means that you might take a look at yourself and what is going on around you. The animals are our guides, our medicine for a more meaningful life."

Thomas eyed her suspiciously.

She went on. "In the folly of the coyote's acts, we can

see our own foolishness. His own tricks always fool him. His humor always backfires. He latches onto a snake thinking it is a bone. He is a signal to us to check our own motives and examine our behavior honestly. Are you playing jokes on yourself, Oscar? Are you conning yourself, on some pathway to foolishness?"

Oscar could not speak. His hand began to quake underneath Jane's. He saw Thomas, open-mouthed, push back his wooden chair from the table and say, "I think I'm going to get us another pitcher of beer."

"You don't have to answer," Jane said quietly to Oscar. "These are only questions you must ask of yourself."

✦

Oscar hid in his room for the next couple of days. He studied the list of the animals and what each signified whenever Thomas wasn't in the room, which was most of the time. Thomas seemed to respect Oscar's need for privacy. Oscar studied the animal characteristics, one by one.

Alligator: Survival, Stealth
Antelope: Speed, Grace
Armadillo: Protection, Safety
Bat: Insight, Intuition
Bear: Strength, Introspection, Self-knowledge
Beaver: Building, Shaping
Bee: Service, Gathering, Community
Buffalo: Abundance, Healing, Good Fortune
Butterfly: Transformation, Balance, Grace
Caribou: Travel, Mobility
Cougar: Balance, Leadership
Coyote: Humor, Trickster, Reversal of Fortune, Folly
Crow: Council, Wisdom, Resourcefulness

Deer: Gentleness, Sensitivity, Peace
Eagle: Potency, Healing, Power, Illumination
Elk: Pride, Power, Majesty
Fox: Cleverness, Subtlety, Discretion
Horse: Freedom, Power, Safe Movement
Hummingbird: Beauty, Wonder, Agility
Lizard: Letting Go, Illusiveness
Loon: Communication, Serenity
Otter: Joy, Laughter, Lightness
Owl: Wisdom, Vision, Insight
Porcupine: Innocence, Humility
Raccoon: Curiosity, Inquisitiveness
Raven: Mystery, Exploration of the Unknown
Roadrunner: Speed, Agility
Skunk: Caution, Warning
Snake: Power, Life Force, Sexual Potency
Spider: Web of Life
Squirrel: Trust, Thrift
Turtle: Love and Protection, Healing, Knowledge
Whale: Creativity, Intuition
Wolf: Teaching Skill, Loyalty, Interdependence
Woodpecker: Change, Persistence

He had gone over the list many times when he heard some commotion in the hall. He heard the sad music of Jane, crying, heard Thomas' low and soothing voice, and heard a knock on his door just as he was beginning the list one more time.

✦

"She's going to need somebody to go with her to the nursing home," Thomas said. "I think her husband's in a bad way."

"Is he going to die?" Oscar said.

"I don't know."

"Where's Daisy?"

Thomas spoke carefully. "I don't know, Oscar. She's going on the bus. You want to go with her?"

"Oh fuck. I don't know. I don't know if I can!"

"I think you can," Thomas said. He nodded down the hall toward Jane's closed door. "She'll be ready to leave in a minute." He started for the stairs. "You're not so old as you think you are, you know. You'll find that out when you have to be strong."

✦

The dream catcher over Jane's husband's bed was even bigger than Oscar's. It was decorated with striped feathers and multi-colored beads, and had a piece of turquoise at its center. She had been quiet on the bus, and was quiet now, holding her sleeping husband's hand and murmuring prayers or words of encouragement that Oscar could not quite understand. He stayed out in a sterile hallway and glanced in every once in awhile. The man seemed to be alive, his chest rose and fell, and he wasn't connected to all of those horrors of technology that Oscar had previously imagined. He was only a sleeping man.

Jane's face turned yellow and wet. She looked up from her husband into space. Her mouth opened slightly and she looked up at the feathered dream catcher and cried without making a noise. She hugged herself and rose from the chair to leave, and as she left her husband there, Oscar saw him open one eye for a moment and then drop off back to sleep. The man's face looked familiar, as if he was a memory of Oscar's, a sepia face in 1938 on the sidewalk outside of his house.

She had been composed, but on the walk out of the nursing home she wilted, crying into a handkerchief, and he took her hand. She threw herself upon him then, crying and trying to kiss him. She smelled gorgeous and he wanted to hold her and to kiss her; she was like a soul magnet.

But he pushed her away, and when a look of shock glazed her eyes, he took her hand again, held it tight, and grounded his feet to the earth to help her home. He stood up straight and was her strength until they got back to the old men's home, where he kissed her forehead and opened the door to her room for her. She nodded her thanks and quietly closed the door.

That night, when he finally went to sleep, Oscar dreamed of field after gold field of butterflies in hues of scarlet, blue, orange, yellow. Their feathery wings caressed his face; they landed on his hands so he could admire them; they flew around his head and made him smile in blissful dizziness. The sun was warm, and he was young and strong, and the sun was still warm when he woke in the morning.

THE SENATOR'S BREAKFAST

The campaign bus is like a big boat on wheels on snow-covered roads, with food, beds, and a bathroom. The senator fogs the passenger window with his breath, his protruding teeth long as a beaver's; he is on the road to running for president. The red, white, and blue bus leans a little on the hairpin turns of rural New Hampshire roads, and his campaign staff yells out whhoooaa! when this happens, especially when it happens at cocktail hour.

The senator's campaign manager is a young woman named Sally. Her strong perfume permeates the upholstery of the bus, and she deftly balances her wine cooler in the plastic cup when they round these turns. Sometimes the bus brushes the overhanging limbs of hardwoods bending in the crisp snow; sometimes the branches snap, and sticks and sparkling wisps of snow cascade past the window.

He always smiles for cameras. A news commentator once referred to him as an idiot savant in tortoise shell glasses, but this didn't bother the senator. It's morning now, and the video crew will be waiting for them. The one thing the Senator feels uncomfortable with, he says to Sally, is having his picture taken. It's a little awkward. It doesn't seem real or right somehow, especially when you're in politics.

"You have to do it," she says, shaking her head. "Now I know you don't like it but you have to do it. Promote, promote, promote." She's holding her cup of coffee, and his, as he brushes his moussed gray hair in place and straightens his tie. An aide to the senator, an intern from Amherst, holds a mirror up for him. "No wonder I don't like the pictures," he says, but he smiles into the mirror. He can never remember the intern's name.

Part of the campaign video crew waits for him in the snow outside Aldena's Diner. Their bodies dance in the cold like ragamuffin soldiers. They rub their arms, dance from toe to toe, rub their arms, and erect tripods in snow-drifts. The senator watches them as the bus pulls up. They become visibly excited and organized at the same time. "Well bless their hearts," says the Senator. Later, when he sees the video, he'll see himself get off the bus and wave to the camera people. He hates to have his picture taken, but for them, it's the least he can do. He pushes himself against the snow to the front door to the diner.

The camera crew is already inside. "There were supposed to be more people in here than this," Sally whispers to him. She doesn't want the mikes to pick up what she says. There is a total of ten New Hampshire people in the diner, six of whom are patrons. The owner is a shapely woman with blue eyes and a strong handshake. "I used to work at the hospital," she says. "Doing the EKGs. Now I own my own business instead." The senator thinks she's beautiful. He is an aesthete. How wonderful she should make such a leap, he thinks, and that she had the courage to do so. There's a proud light in her eyes. He comments into the microphone. "Only in America," he says. "Only in a place like this." He makes the grunting noises.

The video team motions him and Sally to a table at which they've aimed high powered lights and tripod-mounted cameras. "Sit down," they seem to say, without saying anything. The senator looks around a little uncomfortably. Not only will his moving picture be on TV screens across America, but they're planning on doing this as he eats! He's wearing a suit, and none of the other people in the country diner are wearing suits. Sally made him wear it. "That's what candidates do," she had said. "You know that." The patrons in the diner are wearing wool shirts and jeans and overalls.

The camera catches shots of the senator and Sally as he talks to the diner owner, as he walks to the table, as he holds his hand gently over his tie to sit in the straight-backed chair at the table with the red plastic carnation in the vase. He looks around, and sits so upright that his back doesn't touch the back of the chair. He alternates looking at the camera and smiling with watching the diner.

"Well, it certainly is a cold morning here in New Hampshire," says Sally. She puts a paper napkin in her lap.

"It certainly is," says the senator. His eyes roll one way and another and he smiles and looks around. His head is already beginning to sweat under the lights.

"Very woodsy around here, very earthy people."

"Yes, they are," the senator says.

The diner waitress brings glasses of water and an order pad. She looks like a nurse, or someone who works in a hospital, the way she's dressed.

"I'd just like some orange juice and half an English muffin," says Sally. "We already ate once," she says to the camera.

"I'd like some orange juice too. And some coffee. We ate already once this morning," he says to the waitress. "You know how that is."

The waitress doesn't smile. "Regular, or black?" she says.

"Regular?"

"With cream and sugar, or black?"

"Black, please."

When she leaves, the senator cranes his neck and waves to someone across the diner. The camera operator misunderstands and pans over to a stoic old man in overalls and a feed cap who is reading the paper. He doesn't notice the senator. The senator's still grinning when the camera pans back. He rises from the table to greet a newcomer, a young man who has just entered the diner. The man walks in front of the camera and blocks the view of the senator at first, and the video crew whispers loudly to him before he steps to one side. His hair is long and pulled back with a rubber band. He wears tinted glasses.

"Senator!" he says.

"Friendly people here in New Hampshire," says the senator to Sally, as an aside.

"I'm not from New Hampshire, Senator!" says the man. "I'm from Ohio! No kidding! I've been helping out with your campaign in Ohio! And I drove all the way here, to help you now." He shakes the senator's hand. "Name's Dave Ward," he says, and then sits down at the table. "I helped with your campaign in Ohio."

"Well now, isn't that nice?" says the senator.

Sally's quiet.

"I can't believe I'm here with you, man," the Ohio guy says.

The coffee and juice arrive, and the senator leans back in his chair. He smiles and loosens his tie. He slurps his coffee and then his juice, grunting happily.

"I have my own business," Dave says, "I'm in the appliance repair business. And what you want to do for small business sounds very good to me, man."

The senator uses his napkin. "I'm glad you approve. What is it specifically that you like?"

"Well, you don't have a lot of red tape. You want to take the red tape out of owning a business." Dave turns around, and for a moment his face is inches from the camera. "Could I get some coffee?" he says. He turns the other way again and calls out into the diner. "Could I get some coffee or juice or something?" He faces the senator again. "Like I said, employees are a big responsibility, and as a business owner I'd rather spend my time taking care of them than all this red tape bullshit, you know?"

The senator nods and sips his coffee.

Sally says, "Oh look Senator, there are some more people who came in the diner. Think we ought to say hello?"

"Those people were already here," says Dave.

The senator's eyes gaze vaguely to the right. As if he sees nothing there, or forgets what he's looking at, he smiles at Dave again.

"Man, you're not even like a real senator. You're a caring person, who's out for the well being of small business and a growing economy," Dave says.

Sally looks deliberately at the senator and at the camera. "We'd better get going now, Pete. We have an appointment at the house of the New Hampshire campaign chairman."

"Oh yes! Yes. If you'll excuse us," he says, nodding to Dave. He tilts his head all the way back to finish the last drops of his coffee.

As they leave the diner, Sally urges the senator toward the four locals—the man with the newspaper, a young woman with a tired face, and a couple of middle aged men—but nobody really wants to talk to him. They shake his hand and look at their food. The senator glances back at Dave, who waves from his place at the table, and catches sight of Aldena, who has a twinkle in her eye.

✦

At the campaign chairman's house, a very small ranch, the camera crew puts the senator in front of the hearth with the dried flower wreath and the pictures of children. His supporters fill the place, and even the bus driver has come inside, and stands in a corner nursing coffee too hot to drink. The senator's so hot he can feel the pores of his skin opening, feel the thin dress shirt stick and bubble on his back like the skin of a blister.

There are some non-supporters there too, and they asked the senator about morality and religion and the life of the working man. The senator politely ignores these questions. It isn't that he doesn't care about them, but he doesn't know what they mean in terms of his running for president. The people in the house touch him all the time. They pat his back and shoulders and rub up against his upper arms.

He smells cat urine, the *chili con queso* in the crock pot, the salmon spread on the little crackers, faded dime store powders on elderly women. He can feel the radiant human heat in the pink living room, and he swaps sweat with his well-wishers when he shakes their hands. A very old woman who is all bosom wraps her small arms around him in a hug. The heat of the house has run and cracked her foundation make-up, and she looks like an ancient art museum painting. A squirming infant vomits milk onto the diaper on its mother's shoulder. The camera follows him everywhere.

Most are kind, elderly. A woman in her late sixties with a breath fouler than last week's garbage breathes, "I want to know what'll happen to my social security. And how much drugs are going to cost. I saw terrible things on TV." The senator doesn't want to talk to her about drugs. Her eyes are droopy and yellow.

This reminds the senator that the TV in the living room is on, and he glances at it. The current U.S. president is giving a speech, the volume is turned down, and the president moves his thick lips in vain. Old women in wide flowered dresses and men in overalls eating ham salad stagger the senator's view of the president as they pass back and forth in front of the television, oblivious. The senator sees a serious and drawn expression on the president's face, his jaw moving stiffly up and down.

"There won't be any social security a generation from now," the young mother with the baby says. "You people will have spent it."

Droopy eyes shouts suddenly: "It's our money!"

The senator sees through a window that it has begun to snow outside. He yearns to feel the cold air on his face and in his lungs and hair, and looks around for Sally. When he sees her she averts her eyes. The host of the campaign party dodders over to the thermostat and turns up the heat. The video camera follows the senator everywhere. His head becomes light; people look distant and then very near, and his eyes unfocus as if he's dozing when he is not. He puts his hand to a wall to steady himself, and he's still half-smiling. In his hazy perception of things, he looks out the window.

The video later does a voice-over in this part, saying that the senator was contemplating the beauty of New Hampshire, but at this point he is really looking at Dave from Ohio, not knowing quite whether Dave, standing among snow covered maples with a Molsen in his hand, is real or imagined.

Dave has a T-shirt and a navy blue stocking hat on; his large tinted glasses make him look like an owl from a distance. He holds up the Molsen and gestures wildly at the senator to come outside. The senator looks at a man at his elbow who is trying to talk to him, a man who's wearing a wool shirt and a coat. He doesn't hear the man because his heart is drumming inside his head; his knees feel like toothpicks that won't support his weight. Some music starts, "You're a Grand Old Flag," and somewhere in the mass of people the baby starts to cry.

The senator sees the camera operator abandon his camcorder and disappear into the tiny, aqua-tiled bathroom, as if moving in slow motion. As soon as he is well inside, the senator decides to shuffle through the kitchen to the front door. When he opens it, a delicious rush of snowy air surrounds his face, and he stumbles outside. "Come on, Senator!" Dave yells. He's by the bus, jumping up and down. "Come on! We're going!" The bus driver's keys clink in his left hand as he holds them aloft.

"Well! Damn right we are!" the senator replies, smiling. "Damn right! And I'm driving!"

✦

The senator thinks Aldena is from heaven, she dances so well. She smells like eggs and has a round body and small feet, and the tabletop candles are lit, and the juke box is plugged full of quarters; and the snow outside has ceased, the night lapsing clear and bright and peaceful. She holds onto him around his neck, grasping the green bottle of a Molsen behind his left ear. Willie Nelson is singing "Moonlight in Vermont."

Dave from Ohio is playing a quiet game of spades at the counter with a couple of men from nearby towns who own small businesses, mostly farms. His Camel nonfilters burn down all the way, their ashes like snakes in the ceramic ashtray. There are about ten patrons besides Dave from Ohio in the diner, but they don't know the senator's a senator. The only other one who knows he's a senator is Aldena, in his arms, and Aldena doesn't tell anyone; she whispers in his ear, and says she thinks she loves him, and that as far as she's concerned, the election is over. The senator smiles with his eyes closed. He whispers back, "It's over here, it's over now, but only in a place like this."

WORMWOOD

Adam bounced awake to the roar of a Homelite chain saw. He sat up on a rough wool blanket on the top bunk bed.

"I am building a house with God as a foundation!" the pastor shouted. He revved the chain saw, held it over his head, and kicked open the door of the cabin. He stepped inside.

"What's he doing?" Jeff shouted from the bed under Adam's. Adam could feel Jeff sit up. It jostled the bunk.

Big Freddie, the cabin counselor, stirred in his isolated bed. He wrapped himself in his sheets like a mummy and rammed his head under his pillow.

Outside, a dwindling rain and some vanishing lightning signaled the end of a mountain thunderstorm. The lightning flashes illuminated the pastor's face. He was wild-eyed as a Dickens ghost. His glasses were fogged. Tufts of his hair were blown back by wind through the window. Curtains thrashed with extended tassels so electric they resembled the pastor's hair.

After he exited, still yelling and revving the Homelite, a small voice from a corner said: "He does that every year. He thinks it's a hit. Every year I'm glad when I get to go back to sleep. Welcome to Bible camp, boys."

✦

"What brings you to Camp Rockwood, Adam?" said the pastor. He had thick, styled hair today, stiff on the very top of his head.

"My mother wanted me to go to camp," he replied. "I've never been to camp before. She said this one wasn't too expensive. She thinks I'll learn a lot at camp, about science and ecology." There was the sound of snapping twigs behind them. Adam turned around to see who it was, but no one was there.

The pastor pursed his lips. "Does she," he said. He clasped his hands behind his back as they walked down the path to the dining hall. Large tree roots formed a sort of natural stairway down the path. "And what does your father do?"

"Drinks scotch, mostly," said Adam. "He lives in New York." A chipmunk skittered across the trail.

"Well Adam," the pastor said, "your mother is right. You will learn a lot here."

"Yeah. I didn't know this was a Bible camp. I thought the name sounded kind of Indian. Native American."

"Camp Rockwood is a Christian camp," said the pastor. "But at the same time, it has kind of an Indian ring, you're right."

When Adam and the pastor turned the corner into the dining hall, a small boy with red-gold hair came out from behind the chokecherry and followed. His eyes were so blue they glowed. A Clark's nutcracker followed him in the tree branches overhead.

◆

Big Freddie strung a bow and showed Adam how to aim and shoot at a photo of President Clinton, which was tacked to a straw bale about fifty yards away.

"You want to hold your breath for a second, while you aim and let go," said Freddie.

Adam whizzed an arrow over the president's head; over the bales completely. "Who's that little red-haired kid?"

said Adam. "In our cabin."

"Ronald," said Big Freddie. He picked up another arrow. "He's here every summer, all summer. He's a great challenge for us, and at times we wonder why Jesus sent him to us."

Adam sent an arrow into the left ear of the target. "But didn't his parents send him to you?" said Adam.

"He gets sent here by the state," said Freddie. "By the Department of Family Services. We offer to take kids like that." He positioned an arrow on the bow and pulled back on it. When he let it go it speared into the president's nose. "Got him," he said.

✦

"I feel I must share with you a little about Ronald," said Pastor Bob, the next day. He closed his *New Life Bible* and laid it gently on the dining hall steps.

Adam was a little disheartened. They had been going over some things in Genesis, about how God was so amazing that He had created the earth—no, the whole universe, in a day's time. Rabbits, wind, crickets, everything. Owls, thunder, the moon. He did this for man.

"Ronald," Pastor Bob went on, "was not blessed with a stable home life. He lives here during the summertime, and during part of the winter. And unfortunately—" here he paused deliberately "he was also not blessed with , oh, certain functions of reasoning that you, and I, and the other boys have. Do you understand?"

"You mean he's retarded," said Adam. Just then, he looked out over the lake. On the other side he saw Ronald's tiny figure jumping over some rocks at the mouth of a cave, waving his hands in the air.

Pastor Bob took a deep breath and creased his brow. "Well, I wouldn't call it retarded, exactly. But he's just kind of off in a world of his own. There are certain things he'll just never be able to understand." Red ants were gathering on the toe of the pastor's right boot. There was a food stain there that looked like jelly. "This doesn't mean he's a bad guy or anything."

Adam was encouraged. He fingered the sleeves of his camp T-shirt. "He's hanging out with Christians," he said anxiously.

"That's right," said Pastor Bob. "You know, your mother would be amazed at what you've learned already." He smiled.

◆

Ronald dragged Adam outside in the middle of the night and pulled him by the arm up the mountainside. He stood in a clearing and held his fragile hands up to a sky saturated with so many stars that they sparkled his copper hair. "Look Adam!" he said. "It's the Pleiades. You can only enjoy it for a couple of nights this time of year. Pastor Bob won't show you, so I thought I would."

"Why won't Pastor Bob show me?" said Adam.

"Wormwood," Ronald said.

"What?"

"He doesn't think it has anything to do with God," said Ronald, "It's not one of those things God gave us to use. You know." As he said this, glittery stars fell through the sky behind his head like tracers from fireworks. "He can't see the scales on a fish and the feathers on a bird. He just doesn't see it." He spun around looking up at the stars, making himself dizzy. He fell on the ground. "The Pleiades," he said, as a matter of fact. "It's a star cluster."

◆

In the dining hall the next morning, the children ate pancakes and potato pancakes and bacon. The potato pancakes were last night's mashed potatoes, fried. Adam dumped syrup on it all.

All the boys were fidgety, especially the older ones, almost into their teens. Pastor Bob's wife had come for a visit. The boys stared at her dark, black-lined eyes and her short blue dress, particularly when she got up to get some more pancakes for Pastor Bob. She had billowing, bleached hair past her shoulders which she flipped around with jerks of her head. She smiled constantly.

Ronald sat across from Adam, curiously watching Pastor Bob and Freddie at their table. Freddie nervously stroked a two-morning shadow of a beard as he talked to Pastor Bob, who frowned as he speared pieces of bacon with his fork.

Ronald reeked of pine sap, which made for an eclectic assortment of breakfast scents at the table. He had pine needles in his hair. "They're arguing again," he said. "Pastor Bob will say that I shouldn't come back next year because I create problems, and Freddie will say that I have to. Then Pastor Bob will remind Freddie to clean the latrine. It happens every year."

Adam could feel Pastor Bob looking at him. When he turned to look back, Pastor Bob's frown turned into a grin, and he waved.

Adam talked out of one side of his mouth as he chewed. "So do you want to come back?"

"Yeah. I didn't used to want to, 'til I started noticing things, but I want to now. I didn't used to want to," he repeated. "They always talked about my problems and that made me feel bad."

"What things?" Adam watched Jeff waving to the pastor, holding his *New Life Bible*.

"Things. All kinds of things. The Pleiades, the lake, the

bugs that eat the birds when they die. The sap on the trees, the water spiders on the lake. You know."

"No," said Adam, self-righteously. "I don't."

Ronald brushed some of the pine needles off his head. "You don't?" he said.

"No."

"Oh. They said I was subversive. The subversive apostle. But there's a lot to discover." He took a sudden interest in something outside and ran from the table.

Adam was afraid of him and wondered if subversive had anything to do with the verses in his *New Life Bible*. He decided to ask the pastor the next time they could talk, and just the thought of this made him feel better.

✦

It was time for devotions. Thirteen boys walked to the campfire single-file behind Freddie. The boys had devotions every night, but not every night entailed a campfire, and Pastor Bob had built a Big One. It was built like a teepee, and was about the size of a teepee, and as it blazed sparks flew into the air. A night bird screeched in the distance and the fire crackled and spat, and shoes crushed tiny rocks on the ground. Girls shuffled in from their side of the camp laughing quietly and staring with wide eyes across the rising firelight.

Pastor Bob was already there. He had on some kind of a robe and held his *New Life Bible,* and he held a staff.

"Toss a couple more sticks on," he said to Big Freddie.

Freddie mouthed something but the words didn't come out. Then he said, "I'd really like to do the hell devotion this time."

"You can do it next time. Just throw a couple more sticks on the fire."

"That's what you said last time." Freddie looked at the

ground, shaking his head. He had a hand on his hip.

Pastor Bob clapped Freddie on the back. He shook his head and laughed in merriment as if to smooth Big Freddie's ruffled feathers. Then he began devotions.

"Many people ask me about hell," said Pastor Bob. "And make no mistake folks, hell exists. It says so right here in the Bible. Here's what it says. It says Angel Number Three blew his horn, and a mammoth wicked star started falling from the black sky. And after that it flamed up real big like a gigantic torch, and it fell on a third of all of the waters on the earth. The name of the star is Wormwood. A third of the waters became wormwood, and many men died of the water, because it was made bitter. And then a little later it says Angel Number Five blew his horn, and a star fell from the sky to the earth, and he was given the key to the shaft that leads to the bottomless pit." Pastor Bob stopped reading to throw in an aside: "This is hell, folks," he said. "And it says he opened the shaft of the bottomless pit, and smoke like furnace smoke came out, and the sun and the air were black. Black—can you believe that? But that's what's going to happen. And out of the smoke came monster locusts with the powers of scorpions, but they were not to touch the people with the stamp of Jesus on their foreheads, only they were to get everybody else."

Adam looked around at the other boys. Jeff's eyes were riveted to Pastor Bob, and his mouth was open. Ronald was on the edge of the woods with a blanket and a pillow and was eating something from a paper bag. He stretched, lay down and closed his eyes.

"And if you're not hanging out with Christians, guess where you're going, folks?" Pastor Bob asked his young congregation. "You're going right where those unenlightened people are going. You're going straight to hell. It says so right here in this book."

Right then the teepee fire collapsed with a great whooosh; sparks flashing and spiraling upward into the dark. The children sat back a little. It was a magic moment.

◆

After a picturesque picnic on some rocks, Pastor Bob took the boys fishing. Freddie sat around and scowled as usual, picking at his fingernails with a Swiss army knife.

"For we are fishers of men," said Pastor Bob, reeling in a carp. "The way the apostles were. Because that's what we are now," he said, winking at Adam. "We're apostles."

Adam started to grin at him, feeling the pull of God's will to serve and convert others to the truth as God had revealed it to him through Pastor Bob. But then he felt a stronger tug on his line. He surely and steadily reeled in a fish.

It was a bass, with a spiny dorsal fin and a very scaly exterior. Adam held it in his hand and its gills heaved and fell. Its eyes were milky buttons. It flopped in alarm.

A rustling of blue spruce branches and needles caught Adam's attention, and he looked and saw Ronald peering out from among them. His hair shone like a halo in the sun that cascaded through the spruce's branches; his blue eyes were accentuated by the color of the tree.

Ronald pointed to a raven that had landed on a log that spanned the stream. It looked at Adam with a jerky movement of its head. It looked at the fish, and then back at Adam. Then it preened its scaly breast feathers with a wide beak.

Pastor Bob held his arms out in supplication, still talking. "We must all be fishers of men, no matter what it takes. Do not be so in awe of the works of God around you that you do not see what His works within you can do to help others to see the light . . ."

Big Freddie yawned and stretched. He stood and meandered toward the woods.

Ronald pointed to the raven again and nodded. Then he pointed at Adam's fish. Adam gasped. He looked at the fish. Its energy was almost gone. The tail flipped sporadically, raising scales like the feathers on the breast of the raven.

The big raven raised its predator wings and dropped from the branch. It grabbed an open can of Vienna sausages from their picnic in its beak and rose into a cloudless sky.

Adam ripped the hook from the mouth of the bass and tossed it back into the stream. It swam into dark circles of green rock and hid there. When Pastor Bob looked to the heavens for answers, still talking, he eased over to edge of the woods, and then disappeared with Ronald among the pines.

◆

They crossed through shady places carpeted with pine needles and came to the bright dryness of a small canyon. Pine seedlings had sprung miraculously out of sheer rock, and Ronald pointed these out as they went. The wind picked up and ruffled his hair each time he emerged from a crack or a cranny; the main arm of the canyon was like a wind tunnel.

But an eerie noise, almost indistinguishable from the breeze itself, came from upwind. It sounded a little like a tormented animal. The boys faced each other in alarm. Ronald shrugged and gestured for Adam to follow him.

They had only gone about fifty paces, tripping over rocks and disturbing dust, when the direction of the sound changed. It appeared to be coming from a greener recess to their left.

The sound was not an animal in distress. It came from

the pastor's wife, Mrs. Bob. She was in the nook of the canyon with Freddie, who had her backed up against a rock wall and had a hand up her short blue dress. She moaned and squealed and made all kinds of noises, her blinding blonde hair a mass over her face. He had his face buried in her neck, and her head careened back and forth. The boys ascended a steep slope of pink rock to hide behind a boulder and watch. They stared in fascination.

Mrs. Bob subdued her groaning slightly, and Freddie unzipped his pants, and that would have been the beginning of something if it hadn't been for the snake. It was a rattlesnake and blended in with its surroundings so ingeniously and so perfectly that the boys would not have seen it lying still if they'd been looking straight at it. Its colors and markings were identical to those of the surrounding rocks, grasses, trees, and dry dirt. The boys noticed it because it moved. Mrs. Bob and Freddie were of course not looking, but noticed the snake when it started the low rattling sound of the twitching of its tail.

"Shit!" said Freddie. He leaped away from the rattler and ran back down the canyon, kicking up clouds of dirt that the wind whisked away.

Mrs. Bob, on the other hand, was paralyzed. She stayed backed up against the rock, her hands pressed against it, staring at the snake with make-up blackened eyes like silver dollars. Her lips were pressed in a straight line.

Ronald scooted down the steep rock on the butt of his jeans. "Mrs. Bob!" he said.

She looked up with a horror that was worse than that of seeing the snake, and then she watched the snake again. The snake was in the sun and not rattling much, only from time to time.

"Move away from him, but move very slowly the first few steps," Ronald said. "He'll try to jump at you if you move around close to him."

Mrs. Bob stayed glued to the rock.

Ronald moved quietly through sprouting trees and mazes of rock until he overlooked the snake and was about five feet above it. He picked up a heavy, oblong stone and dropped it on the animal, smashing the middle portion of its length. The head and tail protruding from either side of the rock twitched frantically with a hissing sound.

Mrs. Bob was crying. She pulled herself away from the rock finally, and stumbled back down the canyon to camp, the skirt of her blue dress a little wrinkled and covered with dirt from the scuffle.

✦

They didn't see her again until the next day, the last day of camp, when the buses came to take the campers back to town. She was standing with Pastor Bob and had her arm through his, and since they were going back to town too, she wore some very high heeled red shoes. She nodded as Pastor Bob gave the boys some last instructions in apostleship. Big Freddie loaded sleeping bags and backpacks into the opened sides of buses.

Ronald wasn't going back to town on the bus. The state was supposed to pick him up separately and take him to a foster home somewhere. He sat on a rock wall that surrounded the dining hall, dangling his slender legs. Adam approached him and nodded to Mrs. Bob. "Did she say anything to you?" he said.

Ronald looked down at her there, standing on the road. "No," he said. "But she might later on. I'll be back again, next year." When Adam's bus left the camp Ronald was still sitting there, gazing up at the sky and the trees in the mottled sunlight, sniffing the cool mountain air.

AS A HANDYMAN

Patrick was in an uncomfortable position, tangled in the entrails of the kitchen sink, when he went into another seizure. The upper half of his perpetually tired and gangly body was situated in the cabinet area under the counter. What he had of a waist, as well as his legs, which were clothed in very worn and dirty Levis, were on the outside of the cabinet door. They began to twitch, and then to kick and flail violently on the geometrically patterned linoleum floor.

Chase McKeg was in the pink bathroom of the house he was converting to apartments, striking various poses in front of a cracked mirror. His brawny and tan physique contrasted with some a la mode white drawstring pants he had first admired in a kitsch men's fashion magazine. They looked a little like karate pants, but were just different enough to pass off as part of his personality. This is what Chase McKeg intended and how he presented himself.

But he was interrupted by the fracas in the kitchen. He swore aloud and spoke to his own fractured reflection. "What's he doing now?"

Pat's legs were now moving with the forceful percussion of a jack hammer, his tennis shoes pounding the floor rapidly in a kind of rhythm when Chase McKeg entered the kitchen. Even more percussive, though, in a bass sort of way, was the sound his head was making as it pounded the pipes and the plywood floor of the cabinet, out of sight.

Chase stepped over a case of beer he had bought Pat in exchange for fixing the sink. He bent down and pulled on Patrick's legs.

There was some swearing under the sink, and then no more oral noises, just more head-banging, and Chase McKeg came to the conclusion that in order for Patrick's upper body to come out, certain adjustments would have to be made. Patrick had, after all, sidled his upper body under the sink at an angle to avoid the pipes. So Chase McKeg let go of the legs, which immediately resumed their beating and flailing, and angled Patrick's torso out of the cabinet doorway.

Pat's baseball cap clopped to the floor, exposing the shiny baldness that crowned peripheral wisps of long, dishwater blond hair. His wire-rimmed glasses were bent, presumably by the force his head exerted against the pipes; his pale green eyes had rolled back into his head, and his tongue lolled out of a corner of his mouth. He bumped, banged, and hurled himself against the kitchen floor of geometrics.

Chase McKeg was unsettled and annoyed. As he yanked the phone receiver from its cradle to call an ambulance, Patrick suddenly and inexplicably started scratching and ripping at his Levis. He had one leg of them torn almost all the way off by the time Chase McKeg finished the call.

✦

Patrick sat on the edge of the cot in the emergency room and peeled off the adhesive tape from his arm, where it was keeping the IV needle in place. He had his cap on.

"I think you're supposed to wait and have the nurse take that out," said Chase McKeg.

"Naw," said Patrick. He extricated the needle from a

vein in his forearm and let it drop. It dangled and swayed on the end of its plastic hose. "The nurse'll take too long, and then they'll want to know how they're going to get paid and all that. Hand me my shoes, will ya? They're in the gray cabinet behind you." He rolled the tape into a ball between his fingers and let it drop to the sanitized tile floor.

"Anyway, like I said," said Chase McKeg, "if you're feeling good enough we can finish that sink today. I got you another case of beer for your trouble. It's in the car."

Patrick nodded. The two left the hospital without speaking to anyone and without signing any papers. The needle swayed on the plastic hose as if disturbed by a breeze.

✦

Patrick had a five-year-old son that looked nothing like him, and one Tuesday afternoon in the heat of summer Patrick brought Dallas with him to do a roofing job for Chase McKeg.

"He's a knot-head," Patrick said affectionately of his son. Chase guessed that Dallas did not accompany Patrick very often. Patrick was divorced.

Dallas had a small head that was oblong and angular and his black eyes were like rocks. He had very short hair, except for some trailing brown tendrils of it that extended from the base of his neck to the middle of his back. If he had to do something he didn't want to do, or if he was not permitted to do something he did want to do, he would stand upright in his little black and white and red cowboy boots, stiffening his arms at his sides and making fists, and he would drool and growl like a dog.

"His mother used to lock him up in his room," Patrick said to Chase McKeg on such an occasion, as if this explained everything. "She takes him to a shrink now and the shrink gives him drugs."

✦

Dallas sat Indian style in the dry dirt among the shingles. He had already threatened the mongrel dog who lived next door with a splintery two-by-four with projecting nails; when Dallas finally made contact between the spiky nails and the dog's cheek the mutt growled and snapped, and from then on the game lost its magic, because when the dog bared its teeth and snapped so hard that flews flopped and spittle flew, Dallas became suddenly and rudely aware that the game was real. So he balled his fists and growled and drooled at the dog, and then took the embellished board over to a pile of shingles. He threw handfuls of loose dirt into the air and created a cloud of dust that stuck to the drooly spots on his T-shirt and settled into the die-cuts in his cowboy boots, and then he began to spear sparkly black shingles onto the nails on the board. This wasn't as satisfactory as tormenting the dog, and so he was frustrated, but he would soon become engrossed in the spearing and tearing of the twinkling black shingles and forget about the dog. The shingles emitted a tarry fragrance in the Missouri summer sun, and Dallas sniffed them occasionally, and scratched the sparkles on them with his tiny, sharp fingernails.

It was around one o'clock at this point and Patrick had been on the roof for about five hours ripping and laying shingles. The radio in his unlicensed pickup truck had informed him that the high temperature for the day could reach one hundred-two degrees with a humidity of ninety-five percent; he had reminded Chase McKeg that to do the job he would need plenty of beer. But the first twelve pack of Stag was almost gone, and the ice in the Igloo cooler had already melted, and there was a warm-stale beer taste in Patrick's mouth that he could eliminate, he felt, only by drinking another beer.

"Dallas!" Patrick peered over the side of the roof to see the child sitting among the shingles, hammering one board onto another with a rock. He didn't look up. Satisfied that Dallas was safely occupied, Patrick traversed the slope of the roof to where the cooler was, where the ladder butted up against the gutter. He twisted the cap off of a warm Stag, felt rubber-legged for an instant, quaffed some of the beer, and climbed the slope again to resume his work. His sweat-soaked Grateful Dead T-shirt was like an onion skin against his chest and back. He peeled it off and tossed it over the side of the roof. It landed heavily among the shingles like a wet towel, much to the surprise of Dallas.

✦

When the paramedics arrived this time they found Patrick flat on his back on the ground next to a pile of shingles. He had speared himself on the board with the protruding nails but the paramedics didn't notice this until they picked Patrick up.

Dallas held in one hand a large leather wallet that contained a vial of insulin and in the other he held an unused syringe and an empty Stag bottle. He talked to himself like an insidious cartoon character as the paramedics arrived. They took the syringe and the insulin from him.

Chase was trying in vain to pour a Pepsi down Pat's throat, but this wasn't working very well because Patrick was not conscious. The Pepsi ran in rivulets down both beard-stubbled sides of Patrick's mouth and onto the hot dirt. "I couldn't find any orange juice," Chase said to a robust female paramedic. "I got this Pepsi from the guy next door. The last paramedics told me to give him some orange juice with sugar in it, but like I said, I couldn't find any." He smoothed back his blond, moussed hair and wiped his forehead with a monogrammed handkerchief he produced from a pocket of his baggy drawstring pants.

The "guy next door" was a bald, toothless man of around fifty who had been watching the calamity but who now paused to examine the bleeding cheek of his mongrel dog.

After giving both a rolling-eyed sidelong glance, like a horse with its ears back, Dallas threw himself into an exaggerated trot in the direction of his unconscious father.

And the paramedics picked up Patrick and saw what looked like a cross or an X nailed to one side of his back, with some new shingles sandwiched in between wood and flesh.

"It's not sunstroke," said Chase McKeg, brushing some dirt from his white pants. "He's diabetic. That's what the paramedics last time told me. What's that on his back?"

The nails which protruded from the boards were luckily not too long. The large female paramedic pulled them from Patrick's back. Another secured Patrick onto a stretcher.

"I'm sure he'll be calling me to pick him up from the hospital," Chase called after the paramedics. They were taking the stretcher to the ambulance. "Maybe I'll see you there!"

The woman regarded Chase McKeg. "The last thing this man needs is alcohol," she said. It was as if she knew how Pat got paid.

He felt someone pulling on his silk shirt, and he looked down at Dallas, who was now holding the boards.

"Pat's going to the hospital," he said of his father. He spoke with exaggerated immaturity, as if to be cute, and Chase McKeg realized that the child needed a ride back to his mother.

To Chase McKeg, in his silk shirts and white Kung Fu pants, Dallas was revolting. The boy was filthy and displayed a perpetual rivulet of green snot under one or the other of his nostrils, and if he happened to wipe this off with his arm, it created a gap in the thinly resident layer of brown dirt on his face. If Dallas had a tantrum and cried, the streams of tears did the same thing under his eyes. The dirt made him look dark-complected from a distance, until Chase got close enough to realize it was dirt. Dallas was clothed in the worn clothes of white children on welfare, with accessories like Harley Davidson and rock concert iron-on decals.

"Look at my tattoo," said Dallas. The little guy rolled up the sleeve of his oversized Harley Davidson T-shirt to display what there was of a bicep area on his spaghetti-like arm. Around it (since the circumference was not great) was a gigantic, blue-green tattoo—a wormy caterpillar with a smiling, surprisingly human face, with the words LITTLE WILD MAN etched underneath.

Chase thought at first that it was a stick-on tattoo and moved closer to Dallas to try and scratch part of it off, but Dallas winced and pulled away from him. "It hurt like hell when the guy put it on," Dallas said.

Dallas smelled like the monkey house at the zoo, and Chase McKeg did not want the child in his Buick. Yet he realized he'd have to take the boy to his mother; Dallas was only five. Chase McKeg told the him to get in the car.

But Dallas knew his address, to Chase McKeg's surprise, and Chase knew where the apartment was because it was one of the slum tenements he had owned previously. It was only a few blocks away. It was where Patrick lived, almost.

◆

Dallas's home was on the second floor, and he and Chase McKeg stepped over the stiff, bloated body of a rat at the foot of the stairs, whose head was tossed over one shoulder and who seemed to be smiling as if exhilarated in death. Dallas pushed open the door to his mother's apartment . The doorknob was missing.

They entered a dark room showered with beer cans which doubled as a kind of sitting room and kitchen. It contained some broken furniture, a stove and a sink. A bony woman cradled her head in her arms on a steel and linoleum table, in the midst of different receptacles used for ashtrays, one of which was a pot pie tin, where her cigarette butts kept company with greasy carrots and peas and parts of crust and partially gelled chicken in bite-sized pieces. There was also a large bong to one side of her head; it was made of pink plastic and tar colored water was visible within it. The stench of the resinated water suggested that it hadn't been changed in quite some time.

When Dallas brushed the black-gray hair from her face she lifted a head that looked atrophied and wrinkled and focused on him for a minute. "Hey baby," she said. When she smiled she showed gaps of tooth root between her gums and the yellow-green enamel of her teeth. An upper bicuspid was missing altogether. In spite of her deterioration, Chase saw that she had had freckles, luminous eyes and an intelligent expression before she began to degenerate.

He did his best to appear composed in the squalor; he knew there was worse in the back yard, where Pat lived, urinating through a knot hole of his tiny shack, near the murky river. He had lived there since before Chase McKeg had bought and sold the tenement.

"Pat's in the hospital again," Dallas said to his mother.

Then she noticed Chase McKeg, sizing up his silk shirt,

his karate pants, and his trendy leather sandals. "Who are you?" she said, and she performed a coughing jag that ended in her spitting something vile into a quart jar on the table.

"Chase McKeg," Chase said proudly. He held out his hand like a businessman.

She didn't shake it. With delicate fingers she filled a paper cup with water from the sink and walked oddly to the peeling windowsill where there was an enormous terra-cotta flowerpot with a furry African violet plant that overfilled it. The plant's mass in the pot was the circumference of a honeydew melon, and it flowered blood purple blooms the size of quarters. Gold stamens starred the flower centers. Her hands shook as she watered the plant and some of the water spilled onto the plywood floor with a sound that reminded Chase McKeg of the beginning of a piss through the knot hole of Pat's shack in the backyard.

"That guy Pat works for?" she said.

Dallas backed himself up against a wall.

Chase remembered that he had introduced himself. He tried his best to smile at her. "That's the one!" he said, with cheer.

Then he ducked, as the pink plastic bong flew past his left ear and missed it only by an inch or so. The foul black bong water spewed onto his silk shirt and his white karate pants and his sandals, and even a little onto the left corner of his mouth, and the pipe landed somewhere behind him before he was out of the apartment, running down the stairs, and leaping over the rat body on the way to his Buick.

She shrieked at him from a screenless window: "You sonofabitch, if you paid him then maybe I'd get some child support!" and he heard the clatter of some kind of debris (beer cans and pot pie tins maybe) as it hit the roof of his car, but he drove away slowly, as if he didn't notice, a brown-hairy, tan arm hanging out the window and his moussed yellow hair fluttering in the breeze over the earpiece of his Raybans. Dallas's face came to mind briefly, and the cross stuck to the skin of Patrick's back, off-center. But he let those go.

✦

Pat happily attached more of the shingles to the roof he had fallen off of. The cloying heat and humidity of the previous day had subsided and he had remembered to take his insulin—Chase McKeg had reminded him—and there was plenty of icy Stag in the Igloo cooler. Chase McKeg had even promised to give him a little cash for the job and to make him a sandwich. Chase had been timid upon picking him up from the hospital the night before and had waited quietly at the desk while a nurse detached Pat from his IV and got him ready to go.

He lit a filterless Lucky Strike and admired the work he had done so far. The Stag felt good.

But there was a wobbling of the top of the ladder against the gutter—the part of the ladder Patrick could see—and Chase McKeg appeared, and he was not alone.

"This is Howie," said Chase, pointing to a head that was just beginning to emerge over the side of the roof. The little man had on red-framed sunglasses with an earpiece missing, earlobe-length brown hair cut in the shape of a helmet, and as he finally made it completely onto the roof Pat saw—a bottle of Stag in his right hand.

He nodded at Pat, legs bent slightly. "I do trim work, mostly. You should see my Ryobi saw—show it to you sometime." He drained the little bottle of Stag and threw it over the side of the roof.

Chase offered no other explanation other than to roll his

eyes heavenward like a television actor and to disappear over the side of the roof and down the ladder again.

"You're messing up these shingles, pal," said Howie. "But then again, I don't mostly do shingles. I'm a trim work man, mostly." Pat tried to squint through his own, clear glasses in order to see behind the darkness of Howie's. It was not possible.

Pat said, "So what's goin' on?" As a handyman he had always worked alone. As an electrical engineer he had worked with other people but that had been twenty years ago, and not even Chase McKeg knew about that. The Buick chugged down the street, away from the house. It needed a new muffler.

Howie started toward the cooler. "Look, I don't know. Chase wants this job finished. Somebody wants to move in or something," he said over his shoulder. "I don't usually do shingles or anything even like shingles." He pulled forth a frosty Stag and opened it; the sunglasses started to fall off, but he caught them. "But just don't steal my fucking tools and we'll be just fine. Know what I mean?"

By the end of the day the handyman silhouettes—baseball cap Pat's and little Howie's with the bent legs—wavered on the roof against the dark blue Missouri dusk, stag-drunk on the roof, but avoiding each other never the less. Pat had no seizure that day.

✦

In the misery of his little shack, Patrick arranged his tools on a piece of pegboard in perfect order with his favorites on the right hand side—the claw hammer, the ratchet screwdriver, and the level. The claw hammer was substantial and worn and the wood on the handle had been smoothed by his hands. The ratchet screwdriver made a precise noise like the winding of a clock; and the level, though its red paint was chipped in places, was like a miracle to Patrick—the shiny bubble inside setting things straight, he leaned against it for the sense of the rectilinear. His plumb bob was there too, next to the level, but its string was often tangled

And next to his favorite tools, leaning up against the pegboard, was his fishing rod, because on the days when he wasn't drinking with friends or working for Chase McKeg, he borrowed a rowboat and went fishing in hopes of bringing up a bottom feeder, which was about the only kind of fish that survived in the brown-green river. Once when he had been fishing he had looked up, past his shack to the window of his ex-wife's apartment in the big house, and he had seen her staring out and down at him with a vacant expression, as if she were trying to remember something. This had made him glance at the water again and jerk his line a few times, pretending he had gotten a nibble.

✦

When Chase McKeg drove his Buick once again to visit the site of the roofing job, little Howie was ripping and laying the shingles in weather that was like a steam bath. Howie was without a shirt and was wearing shorts and his red-rimmed glasses, and he had pulled what he could of his helmet-cut hair into a short ponytail.

He turned and scowled at Chase McKeg when Chase surmounted the ladder to the roof. Then he went back to his hammering.

"Where's Patrick?" said Chase McKeg.

Howie swore to himself for the benefit of Chase McKeg. He stopped hammering and looked at Chase again. "Why didn't you tell me the guy was epileptic?"

"He's not," said Chase McKeg.

"The hell he ain't," said Howie. "Thief too. Stole my tape measure." He put the hammer down where it made a sandy sound on the new shingles, and stretched, and then pulled a cigarette pack from the pocket of his cut-offs. "But I'll get it back. Happens all the time. People always stealing my fucking tools. I just about knocked old Patrick's lights out." The heavy, hot air made sweat run down his face and upper body constantly, in streams.

"What do you mean?" said Chase McKeg. "Where's Pat?"

Howie lit the cigarette and took a deep drag. "Well, right when I was about to knock his lights out, when he was denying taking the tape measure and all—and denying taking the last beer, by the way—he crumples and starts flipping out in some kind of a seizure or something. Some kind of—fit." He started to laugh quietly, and then to laugh louder. He took off his sunglasses and wiped his eyes. "And then, in the middle of this thing, he rolls off the roof! He flips around and wiggles and rolls off the fucking roof! And then he's gone! He's there, and then, he's not!" Howie laughed himself breathless before he could calm himself. He wiped his eyes again, put his glasses back on, and pulled in some more smoke. "Speaking of beer, Chase, do you happen to have another twelve in that Buick of yours? I figure I got about two more hours on this job, tops. If I could get my check today, that'd be lovely too."

Chase McKeg looked at the side of the roof he thought Patrick must have fallen off of, the same one he fell off of the last time. "Is he in the hospital?"

"Yeah. Somebody called the hospital I guess. A guy with no teeth and an ugly dog. An ambulance came and got him."

Chase McKeg was climbing down the ladder before Howie could finish the explanation. He stopped briefly only to notice a tape measure lying haphazardly in the gutter. Then he proceeded down the ladder to the ground.

✦

"Chase McKeg," Chase said to the nurse at the counter. "I'm here to see Patrick, take him home if he's ready. How is he, incidentally? He's all right, basically, isn't he?"

The nurse looked old and tired. She sighed. "I'll tell him you're here."

When she came back she gestured vaguely to the rows of curtained-off cots. "He's back there. Third one back."

The cot was rumpled, but empty. A ball of sterile adhesive tape lay on the floor, and the IV needle swayed back and forth on the end of a dangling hose.

✦

"How should I know where he is?" Patrick's ex-wife said. "I thought you learned your lesson not to come around here no more!" She sat in the same chair as in Chase McKeg's previous visit, but she was drinking vodka and unable to get up. Outside, it started to rain.

With his rock eyes, Dallas watched from a corner at first, and then clomped over to the sink in his cowboy boots. He filled a dirty glass with water and took it to the African violet. Parting the fuzzy leaves and stems with his steady fingers, he was careful to water only the dirt, which he did slowly and cautiously. Not a drop of water hit the floor. And just as tentatively, behind his mother as she squinted at Chase McKeg, he pointed out the window to the river.

✦

Patrick sat in a painted canoe that had seen better days on the far side of the river in the rain. He was fishing.

Chase McKeg stood by the shack. "Patrick!" he cried. "Glad to see you're okay! Pat!"

Pat did not respond.

The rain was steady and cool. It heightened the fragrance of the blossoms on the locust trees. It showered Pat softly on his arms and his back and his baseball cap. Though it wasn't yet dark, a chuck-will's-widow called from somewhere up and across the stream, muffled by the moisture of the early evening.

"Pat! I got a case in the car! Let's ice 'er up! "

Patrick checked his line and plunked it back into the water again.

"It's Budweiser, Pat! Ice cold Bud!" Chase McKeg yelled.

Pat looked up. He smiled at Chase McKeg, put his rod down and picked up a paddle to guide the canoe to the stronger current somewhere near the middle of the stream. Then he tipped his hat, and he floated down the river in the rain.